# INTO THE
# UNKNOWN

# WHAT OTHERS ARE SAYING . . .

Seven Short Stories of Faith and Bravery

# INTO THE UNKNOWN

*An Ambassador International
Science Fiction Anthology*

**Daniel Peyton**  **Lauren Smyth**
**Eric Landfried**  **Allen Steadham**
**Daphne Self**  **P.S. Patton**
**Jake Tyson**

## AMBASSADOR INTERNATIONAL
GREENVILLE, SOUTH CAROLINA & BELFAST, NORTHERN IRELAND

www.ambassador-international.com

# Into the Unknown

ISBN: 978-1-64960-576-4, Hardcover
ISBN: 978-1-64960-134-6, Paperback
eISBN: 978-1-64960-184-1

Cover design by DM Designs
Interior Typesetting by Dentelle Design

This is a work of fiction. Names, characters, and incidents are all products of the author's imagination or are used for fictional purposes. Any resemblance to actual events or persons, living or dead, is entirely coincidental. Any mentioned brand names, places, and trademarks remain the property of their respective owners, bear no association with the author or the publisher, and are used for fictional purposes only.

Scripture taken from the King James Version of the Holy Bible. Public Domain.

Scripture taken from the New King James Version®. Copyright © 1982 by Thomas Nelson. Used by permission. All rights reserved.

Scripture taken from THE HOLY BIBLE, NEW INTERNATIONAL VERSION®, NIV® Copyright © 1973, 1978, 1984, 2011 by Biblica, Inc.® Used by permission. All rights reserved worldwide.

AMBASSADOR INTERNATIONAL
Emerald House
411 University Ridge, Suite B14
Greenville, SC 29601
United States
www.ambassador-international.com

AMBASSADOR BOOKS
The Mount
2 Woodstock Link
Belfast, BT6 8DD
Northern Ireland, United Kingdom
www.ambassadormedia.co.uk

*The colophon is a trademark of Ambassador, a Christian publishing company.*

# TABLE OF CONTENTS

# Glossary

**Federated Nations**: Planets, countries, and colonies from various regions within the galaxy who work in coordination to provide a centralized government and still retain their sovereignty.

**Science Conglomerate:** Corporations and research facilities joined together to explore and research the unknown regions of the galaxy within the Federated Nations borders.

**Judicial Clerical Court:** Historians who keep a detailed and unbiased record of history, which is recorded in various perspectives. They eventually became purveyors of justice, judging and punishing violent offenders within the Federated Nations borders. The order determines the duty performed. Judicial Clerical Court is also known for its benevolence.
- Zed Order (the highest order): Justice/Judge
- Gamma Order: Patrol/Recorder
- Delta Order: Curator/Custodian of the Clerical Court

**Protocol Alpha:** A moon orbiting a gas giant and the main base for the Judicial Clerical Court.

**Alpha Prime:** Capital of Protocol Alpha

**Null:** the empty, black space before systems are reached

**In-between:** "subspace"; between dimensional planes

*Deep in the black expanse of space, Dr. Tony Henderson discovers a strange anomaly. Seeking answers leads him to a colony and into a decades-old conspiracy.*

.

# ASTRO MISSIONARY

## DANIEL PEYTON

# CHAPTER ONE
## PREPARATIONS

"Hold it! Hold it!" Tony quickly pressed the welder's torch up against the side. A spray of sparks showered two people below him, one had a little fire start on his shirt. Neither person stopped holding the giant metal panel in place. "Got it!"

The two people stepped back and looked up, their auto-sensor eyes running over the device. One announced. "It meets specifications. Measurements established. Retrieving alloy polymer."

Tony jumped down from his perch and met the other person. "So, 865, what do you think?"

The robot looked at the massive device resting in the bay. "The HRN14 meets required standards."

"I didn't ask for your opinion on its standards. I spent the past two months in here getting this ready. It may meet the standards of the previous thirteen versions, but there is a lot of me in this."

865's head jerked side to side as he examined the massive device. "I do not detect any organic compounds within the structural or operational aspects of the HRN14. Please, explain. How are you connected to this device physically?"

Tony rolled his eyes. "Fine, I just have a little more human affection for this device."

"I do not entirely understand."

"You don't have to. Now . . . "

Just then a voice came over the comm. "Hey, Tony, ya wanted to know when we're dropping out of the in-between. The nebula is off our nose right now."

"Gotcha, Roger. I'll have the HRN ready to launch."

"Good. Bridge out."

Tony wiped his hands on a rag. "Okay, 899, grab 888 and 854 and get this thing in the launch tube. 865, let's go see that nebula."

"Understood." 865 stiffly walked with him out of the bay while three other, nearly identical robots, went to work with the massive device.

Tony and 865 stepped out of the engineering section and walked around a wide deck. To one side was a line of doors leading to various rooms. A long window replaced the other wall, giving a spectacular view of space.

"Wow!" Tony stopped and leaned against a rail beside the window. His eyes were aglow with reds, blues, and some pinks.

Beyond the window was a nebula. This cloud of gasses burned with dazzling colors. Pillars of cloud burst up through the mass, light shone inside the denser pockets. Swirling areas of the gas surrounded orbs that were slowly becoming stars.

865 scanned the view with jerking motions of his head. "Nebula 74075, the Henderson Nebula, named for astronomer David Henderson in 2245."

"Yes, I know that. David Henderson was my ancestor. Trust me, my father never let me forget all his accomplishments. Right now, I just want to enjoy the view."

865 frowned and continued to scan. "Viewing complete. Locating target parameters should be next objective."

"Viewing isn't complete. I'm still enjoying myself. This is simply amazing."

"You have viewed nebula in holographic re-creations and pictorial reference guides during your education in the academy. How is this different?"

Tony smiled as he watched a puff of orange gasses go by. "It just is. Seeing something that is real is . . . well . . . it's special. It is seeing God's work right in front of your face. Pictures and holograms aren't real; they're just re-creations. This," he gestured to the clouds, "this we cannot create."

865 spent a moment processing, evidenced by the quick motions of his eyes and still silence. Finally, he looked up and cocked his head. "Scientific evidence shows that elements in space created this nebula and gathered due to gravitational forces, energy . . . " He stopped when Tony held up his hand.

"I know what the textbooks say. But I also know that the reality is God made this universe, and the evidence speaks for itself. This— this right here— is the nature of God. We've been studying this stuff for centuries and barely scratched the surface. How can we be so arrogant to think we can explain it when we also admit we hardly know about it?"

"That is a contradicting statement."

"I know, and that's the problem with most science when it comes to understanding God."

865 frowned and dove into his calculations again. After a moment he looked up and said, "Please, explain the nature of God."

Tony laughed hard for a good few minutes, all the while confounding his otherwise coldly logical companion.

After calming down he said, "865, if my father couldn't turn me into a missionary, I certainly ain't starting that job by evangelizing a robot. Trust me. Now, as you said, we need to get those calculations in order for launch. Come on."

He walked onward down the corridor.

865 lost that curious look and returned to his sterile expression. He followed without any further deep questions.

# CHAPTER TWO
# EXPANDING KNOWLEDGE

Tony stood on the bridge next to the captain's chair. Both watched the large monitor as the ship waited near the edge of the nebula.

Captain Roger Ham asked, "Are you certain this nebula will produce enough radiation to power this thing?"

"Yes. In fact, it's emitting three times the solar radiation needed to operate the collectors on the HRN14."

"Good. Is it ready for launch?"

Tony walked back to the science station and checked the readings. "All calculations are a go. It is in launch bay four."

"Send her out."

Tony put the commands in, and the young man at the tactical station launched. Everyone on the bridge watched carefully as the cylindrical device blasted away from the ship. A series of panels ejected, and two large wings opened, spreading the array of Type-40 solar collector cells. Little jets blasted at precise intervals to slow its approach and turn it into the proper direction. Finally, the nose cone on the device popped off and floated away. This revealed the large tube with a lens.

Tony looked at his sensors. "And it's in place."

"Contact Science Conglomerate Base Five," the Captain said.

The comm officer spent a moment at her station and then said, "Doctor Riley is on line one."

"Put her through."

The screen changed from the glorious image of the nebula to that of an older Indian woman with a lab coat on. She had a bright smile and a pair of glasses perched on her nose. "*SCS Polaris,* hello from the Base Five. Our computers have already picked up the connection to the new telescope. We're receiving data on the mainstream now. Gentlemen, you are to be congratulated. You've placed a Hubble Relay Network telescope at the furthest point in human history. With this we can see further than ever before. Mapping uncharted sectors will expand our ability to explore space in ways unthinkable just a few short years ago. And you, Dr. Henderson, should feel proud. You're a part of this moment of history, much as your ancestor was a part of the earliest explorations into deep space."

Tony blushed. "No big deal. We've been explorers for a long time. It's in the blood."

"I believe that. Now . . . wait just a moment." She looked to the side as another scientist showed her a computer tablet. She gave a quick nod and then returned, "It looks like the early data has already proven useful. We're detecting some strange emissions from an uncharted star system not too far from your location. Since this mission is now complete, please head to these coordinates and investigate."

"Ma'am, I'm excited about new discoveries. However, we've been out for a few weeks getting this ready. My crew is ready to head back to a base before going on another mission." Captain Ham said.

"We understand. This will only be an info gathering mission. Swing by the system, launch a few probes, and gather data. It shouldn't add more than two days to your journey. When you return, we will compensate you for the extra time in space."

Captain Ham looked around at his crew. "I suppose we could all use a little extra credits in the bank. Okay, we accept."

"I will connect an uplink to the HRN14 to get the data about the location." Tony replied.

"Good and thank you. Base Five out." The screen shut off.

Tony huffed and walked over to Captain Ham. "Really? More time out here?"

"Just a couple days. Besides, this is a Science ship, exploration is part of everyone's blood around here. Hauling a relay telescope across space wasn't all that much fun for the rest of us. You got to work with it. We just sat and twiddled our thumbs. I, for one, would like to see something interesting and do a little exploration. But, if you want me to change my mind, I can send a cancellation on this and have them send another ship out to investigate this."

Tony rolled his eyes. "No, let's go exploring. Sheesh, nothing's worse than a whiny captain."

"Maybe a lazy scientist." Captain Ham shot back.

Tony scoffed, laughed, and then left the bridge to head for the main science labs.

The astrophysics laboratory flickered in colored light as the various images floated across the screens. Between the computers displaying actual images were screens depicting dazzling calculations being processed by the systems. In the middle of the information hurricane sat Tony. Around him swarmed five robot assistants.

865, his personal assistant, walked over with a computer tablet. "Here is the data from the last processing time."

Tony took the tablet and looked it over. "I see. So, we haven't scanned this part of space often. I wonder why?"

Ignorant of the process of rhetorical questions, 865 answered. "Data indicates that all the information necessary has been gathered. The system in question was too far away from observational systems to continue studying."

"Yes. I know. But it still seems a little illogical that we scanned this system, found curious data, and then simply filed that away. If HRN14 hadn't happened upon this system in its initial scanning radius, we might never have returned to it."

"I do not have a proper answer to that inquiry. I shall seek more information from the computer systems." 865 walked away.

"Hey, no . . . I don't . . . " He couldn't stop 865 from leaving the room. "Go ahead, fine, don't listen to me."

Before the doors of the lab could close, Captain Roger Ham walked in, a curious look on his face. "What is 865 doing?"

"His normal shtick. Always answering questions I don't ask. But I can't fault him, he's loyal."

Roger approached Tony. "True. You programmed him, so I suppose you have only yourself to blame."

Tony laughed. "If only I could create a sense of humor."

Roger looked around at all the data. "All this is focused on that one system they're sending us to?"

"Yup. I pulled everything from the archives and what HRN14 picked up. There is loads of data, but still an unclear picture."

Roger picked up a tablet. "So . . . what's the problem? It looks like another basic solar system with seven planets. Nothing habitable."

Tony turned in his seat and accessed the main computer. The largest monitor in the room flickered on to show the system data. "Some star systems have the Goldilocks zone. This is where a planet can support water and thus life. It doesn't get too hot or too cold."

"Yes, I took basic astronomy in command school." Roger leaned back against a different console.

"Okay, then look at this." The screen focused on a planet in orbit of the star, as re-created by a computer-generated image. "This planet is in the perfect Goldilocks zone."

"Sure, but it's a gas giant. It can't support life . . . at least not life as we've ever discovered."

Tony put a small window within the image, showing a barrage of numbers. "There is one problem, and this is what caused so much curiosity. That planet does not measure as a gas giant. It doesn't create the proper gravitational waves, the radio and ultra-light emissions are all off, and the orbit is too fast. Frankly, it's too close to a star that size to not have either been absorbed or crashed into it at some point. This gas giant goes against nearly ever iota of information we have on gas giants."

"Really? That's interesting."

"What's more interesting . . . everything I just told you, the Science Conglomerate has already known for years. They first read this data when they put the HRN8 in operation. Why haven't we gone after it to investigate? Why did this get quietly filed away and ignored?"

Roger shrugged. "Maybe because it's outside the boundaries of the Federated Space."

"It's in unclaimed space, which is open game for science exploration."

Roger smiled. "Well, I don't know why it wasn't investigated already, but we're going to get that chance now. So, stop fussing about what didn't happen and get ready for what we're gonna do. Might put your name in the history books again."

"Sure. Just what I want."

Roger reached over and shut off the primary screen. "What I want to know is if you can explain another scientific curiosity for me."

"What?" Tony picked up a computer tablet, ready to pull up any data he might need.

"Why you canceled that date I set up for you." Roger said.

Tony, already calling up the search engine, slowly lowered the tablet. "This isn't scientific."

"Oh, yes, it is. I've never met a creature who dodges courting opportunities like you. I mean, seriously, you aren't bad looking, you're only twenty-eight, and you have time. Jennifer was eager to see you, and you stood her up."

"I did not. I sent her a message telling her I was busy at least half an hour before the date. Besides, all you had us doing is eating dinner in the mess. Big deal."

"Yes, big deal. Since we were in grad school together, you've dodged every girl who has shown an interest. You bury yourself in work and pretend like that's all life offers." He leaned back and smirked. "You do like girls . . . right?"

"Yes. I like girls. But you see . . . I've always struggled. I never got a girl to go out with me once. I realized that maybe God designed me to be alone. So, I decided to stay that way."

"Fine, I'll leave it between you and God. But don't be too surprised if the Almighty throws you a curveball one of these days and you fall for some girl."

"Sure. Now, I want to get back to this."

Roger left as he said, "Don't stay up all night."

# CHAPTER THREE
## GOLDILOCKS ZONE

Tony staggered out of the lift doors, a steaming cup of coffee in one hand. He made his way to the science station and pulled the seat out from the wall. Plopping down, he quickly drank more of the coffee and then leaned his head back.

Roger turned his chair around. "You look like death warmed over. I know you're not a morning person, but do you have a hangover?"

Tony didn't lift his head to answer. "You know I don't drink. I was up until five a.m. studying all the data coming in from HRN14 about this solar system."

"Seriously? You know I said we would stop by and have a look. You don't have to do this to yourself."

"You've known me for twenty years. When I get a thought in my head, I have to run with it. Something about this data is bothering me."

Roger shook his head. "Could be that there's nothing special about this solar system. Just another non-habitable system with a gas giant in the Goldilocks zone."

"If that's the case, then HRN14 is faulty, and that would really grind on me. I worked too long on that telescope to have it mess up like this."

Just then the boy at helm said, "Approaching coordinates."

Roger smiled. "Well, we're about to find out one way or another." He turned back around and gave his orders. "Helm, take us back to normal space."

Tony perked up as much as he could and quickly activated his station. "I have the sensors on hot."

"Good. We can't spend too much time here."

Helm announced, "Entering normal space."

All eyes turned to the screen as the blur of bright colors broke like coming through a dense fog bank into a night sky. At the center of this was a bright star with planets in orbit.

The *Polaris* flew toward the bright yellowish white star. From this distance they could already see several colorful gas giants in orbit.

"Helm, ETA to the Goldilocks zone at surveying speeds?"

"Five hours, seven minutes."

Roger turned his seat around. "Is that enough time? We can't spend much more than that."

Tony had his face buried in the screens. He said nothing.

"Hello, Tony, wake up."

Tony shook his head. "This . . . can't be right."

"What?" Roger got up and joined his friend.

Tony pressed several buttons and changed the readings. "If my scans are showing me the right data, I'm not picking up that gas giant at all."

"Is there a planet there?"

Tony slowly nodded as he checked more readings. "It looks like an exoplanet, and it is Earth sized."

Roger leaned over and pointed at another readout. "Look, we're picking up radio waves, artificial energy signatures. Can we detect life on this planet?"

"We need to get closer to be sure about life readings. I'm reading organic material, but that could be moss."

"Moss doesn't emit radio waves," Roger stated.

"Sir!" The young woman at comm called out. "We're receiving a transmission."

Roger and Tony looked at one another in shock. "Is it coming from that planet?" Roger asked.

"No, sir. It's coming from null space. It is an automated signal."

"Put it through." Roger returned to his seat.

A voice came over the comm. "You have entered a restricted area. Turn your ship around and return to Federated Nations Space. You have entered a restricted area. Turn your ship around and return to Federated Nations Space. You have . . . " The transmission cut when Roger gave a swipe motion across his throat.

Tony frowned. "The FN doesn't have anything out here. This is unclaimed space."

"Where did that originate from?" Roger asked.

The comm officer checked her systems. "I'm picking up a buoy within the border of FN space."

Tony turned to Roger. "Could this be a warning to outsiders entering our space?"

Roger dove into a moment of thought. The bridge fell silent as the captain pondered this. Finally, he said, "I don't know. The sectors near here aren't exactly strategic sites. Most of them are null space or uninhabited systems. We welcome visitors to our space all the time. It feels like this is warning us about entering this system."

"What could this mean?" Tony asked.

Roger gave this more thought. "Back, during the war with the Kalshon, the Kalshon would hijack our security satellites to make it appear sectors were ours, so our ships would fall into ambushes. This could be a similar situation. Someone might be using one of our security satellites to make outsiders believe this system is Federated space."

"Then they could be peaceful and just want to be left alone." Tony said.

"Maybe. But I don't like anyone using our tech for their purposes without our permission. If these people here want Federated protection, they can join."

"Then we keep investigating?"

"Yes. This is more important now. My superiors will want to know about this. Helm, continue on course, just be ready to jump back into subspace in case these people don't take kindly to our presence."

"Aye, sir."

Tony sat at his seat in the astrophysics lab. In front of him was a massive screen displaying the view in front of the ship outside. They zoomed through this solar system, passing beautiful gas giants, amazing icy moons, and one extremely volcanic planet that had a ring of dust around it that shimmered in purple hues.

Robot 865 walked in with a tray. He carefully set it on the console near Tony.

Tony changed the view with a swipe of his hand. The image zoomed in on a moon that had a starkly green surface. As his eyes marveled at the view, he casually asked, "What's this?"

"Sustenance, sir. You haven't eaten in more than seven hours. The human body requires metabolic fuel in the form of food intake," 865 stated.

Tony ran this green moon through his sensors. "Sorry I missed lunch; was working hard on this project. We don't have a lot of time."

"And you missed breakfast this morning, sir. You only consumed four cups of coffee, which does not contain a high caloric content."

"I didn't know you were keeping track."

865 walked over to a station near the wall. "You asked me to help you during this mission. Monitoring your health qualifies as help. Or am I mistaken, sir?"

"I suppose it does." He changed the monitor again. "Just moss."

"The food content I brought you does not contain any bryophyta elements."

Tony laughed. "I was talking about the moon. It was green and contained a high level of oxygen. However, the oxygen content is at toxic levels for most living creatures. It produces the oxygen in a strange moss-like plant that covers nearly the entire surface. Might be worth exploring at a later time."

"Understood."

Tony sat back and rubbed his temples. "Yeah, I'm getting that headache that's telling me I need to eat something. Let's see what you brought me." He took the top off the tray and found a simple meal from the basic nutrition stores. A bag of dried apple slices, a packet of seasoned tuna, a piece of flat-bread, and a pack of vitamin infused water. "Ah, nutrition selection three. My favorite of the five to choose from."

"I know. You selected this option more than eighty percent of the time during work on the HRN14 during transit."

"Glad you paid attention. Thanks." He ripped open the tuna packet and squeezed it over the flat bread. He had just chomped down when the sensors went wild.

865 announced, "Life detected on monitoring station one."

Tony quickly checked his scans and then put a new image up on the main viewer. A planet sat before them with green and brown continents and blue oceans. Storm clouds moved in bands, and bluish-white ice caps dominated both the north and south poles.

"It's beautiful."

"It is a standard habitable planet with an Earth-like atmosphere. Pollutant particles are far less dense than normal industrialized planets inhabited by humanoid life forms," 865 stated.

Tony, still eating his lunch, worked furiously at his console. "Check for signs of advanced life forms. I'm not seeing any orbital space traffic of any nature, not even satellites."

865 activated a window within the primary screen to display the readings. "Sensors indicate evidence of advanced life-forms. There is an indication of construction and composite alloys. Energy readings are showing class seven energy generation."

Tony frowned. "Class seven. But that would be modern. They're using sub-nuclear power generators, just like our ship. I want the main sensors to scan for these life-forms. They might be a small settlement. Though a settlement in unclaimed space is risky."

"Conducting scans."

Tony checked his sensors. "I'm picking up a strange energy wave coming from an emitter in the magnetic north pole. It's artificial. This looks like . . . an emergency signal, but . . . wait, this is creating a looping wave. This is creating the illusion of a gas giant. How odd."

"Sensor readings confirm life-form readings are human," 865 announced.

"I know they are humanoid . . . "

"No, sir, human. Sensors clearly indicate that life-forms are human, from the Terran solar system."

Tony slowed down his frenetic work. "Humans . . . . Out here. There aren't any colonies past Brikka Major."

"Should we send a probe to conduct a closer investigation?" 865 asked.

"No. I need to talk to Captain Ham about this. This changes everything." Tony quickly left his station behind and ran for the door.

Tony burst through the lift doors and rushed up to the captain. "Sir, we have a problem."

"I was just about to contact you. What sort of problem?"

Tony pointed at the planet on the main view screen. "There are humans down there."

"Humans? There can't be. All human colonies are registered with the Judicial Court. We have nothing beyond Brikka Major, at least I think that's the extent of colonization. Besides, this is unclaimed space. No one would be stupid enough to establish a colony in unclaimed space."

"I have another theory," Tony said. "I discovered the signal that confused our readings. They're sending an emergency signal that is looping. Instead of calling for help, it causes the magnetic poles of this planet to distort long-range detection."

"What is your theory then?"

Tony looked up at the screen. "Someone crashed here and sent a distress call. But it's distorted, and no one realized they needed help."

"If that's true, then these people have spent decades hoping for rescue. Are you sure about that theory?"

"Almost."

"Almost?"

"The only problem I have is that we're detecting evidence of energy patterns from extremely modern systems. If a ship crashed here twenty or more years ago, they wouldn't have these kinds of energies, not yet."

"There is one way to find out. Comm, send a standard greeting, see if anyone down there picks up on it," Roger said.

The communications officer sent out the signal, which came across in four hundred basic languages. After a moment she looked up. "Sir, I am detecting a reception of this signal, but they aren't responding."

"They might not be able to," Tony added.

Roger mulled this over for a moment. "This will put us behind, but we have to know. Tony, I'm going to send you down with your robot and a small team of security. Contact these humans."

"Me?"

"I think sending a scientist down might be better than just security. If they don't want us there, we will leave. If they need help, you can assess the situation and bring the information back to me. Let them know we're only a science vessel and not equipped for a mass rescue operation. However, we'll contact the nearest military base, and they can coordinate a rescue."

"I'm no diplomat."

Roger smiled. "You are the son of a preacher and missionary; you're good at talking to strangers and making them feel comfortable. That makes you the closest thing we have to a diplomat on a science vessel. Now, we don't have time to argue. This will already put us behind schedule, and I don't want to annoy our superiors any more than we have to. Get going."

"Aye, aye, Captain."

# CHAPTER FOUR
# FRIENDLY NATIVES

The shuttle lowered through a light layer of clouds and then landed in a grassy opening in the middle of a lush forest.

Tony turned off the atmospheric controls. Then swiveled around to look at the others. There were two burly men with gray and black uniforms on, and 865 waiting with his ever-present look of curiosity.

"Okay, this is only a fact-finding mission. No weapons yet. Stay near in case of unfriendly wildlife. Our mission is to find and contact the humans living on this world. Now . . . " The lights flickered and dimmed. "What?" Tony turned back around.

"Is something wrong?" Charlie asked.

"The batteries are drained, almost dead. That's odd. Must have not been properly charged before leaving the dock. I'll open the solar collectors; they'll be fine." He returned to his people. "Okay, let's move out. 865, I want you to keep a constant visual recording at highest detail."

"Understood." 865 blinked and his eyes beamed a blue light.

The team left the shuttle with Tony at the lead. The two security personnel walked close, always keeping a strict watch. Neither held their weapons, but their hands were poised for action. 865 turned his head left to right, to left to right, as he recorded.

They had walked at least half an hour when Tony stopped. "This is odd."

Charlie already had his gun out. "What?"

"Put that away. What I meant is my scanner is powering down. Its battery is dead. But it can't be. I just took it off the charging station. 865 could you . . ." Suddenly the robot flopped to the ground in a dead heap. "What?"

"Sir, our weapons. They're powering down too." Bill, the other officer, shook his gun.

Tony quickly waved to the ship. "Bill, get 865 back to the shuttle and signal the *Polaris*. I think we might have discovered the problem down here. Some kind of energy dampening field."

"Shouldn't we all go back?" Charlie asked.

"No. I still want to find these humans. You two, head back. Charlie, you're with me."

Bill scooped up the robot and slung him over a shoulder. Tony and Charlie pressed on.

Bill dropped the floppy robot on the floor of the shuttle and rushed to the comm station. Every light and panel flickered and faded. A garbled, slow voice from the computer spoke, but it was not clear.

He punched the comm button. "*Polaris*, do you copy?"

Nothing.

"*Polaris*, this is Shuttle Two, do you copy?"

Nothing.

Just then a banging rang out from the back door. Someone or something was trying to open it. Bill pulled his gun, then realized it was of no use. He tossed it aside and prepared himself for martial combat. A creaking sound echoed, and the door opened.

"How are you scanning, sir?" Charlie asked.

"With my eyes, ears, nose, and touch. The most ancient way God designed us to learn. Though I'd like to record this in something other than my brain." Tony said.

They moved through the trees, marveling at the unique foliage of this world. Stunning flowers, vines that grew so fast they could see the movement, a bird that yelled like a myotonic goat. Most odd was that the planet spun in the opposite direction of Earth.

Finally, they left the trees for a much more open area. Rolling, grassy hills spread out before them and led up to tall, snowy mountains.

"Wow, I guess they could have found a worse place to crash-land," Tony stated.

"It is amazing, sir. But . . . " Charlie jumped and partly covered Tony.

"What are you doing?" Tony shoved at the man holding him.

Charlie quietly surveyed the area with an intense glare. "I heard something. Movement."

"Probably an animal. Stay calm."

"Maybe, sir. I . . . watch out!"

Just then a team of strange-looking people rushed over the hills. They appeared as human, but with odd metallic patches on their skin. Each person had the same arrangement, a plate of metal over one eye, a plate of metal on each upper arm. Metal hands and small plates attached to their forearms.

One man grabbed Tony immediately and punched him, sending him sprawling across the ground. Charlie didn't go down so quickly. He met their attacks with precise counterattacks, blocked hits, threw one man, nailed one woman in the gut with his foot, and dodged two others. In the end, they caught him by the arms and then broke his leg.

"Who are you?" A woman yelled.

Tony, now being pressed to the ground with a foot on his chest, said, "I'm Dr. Tony Henderson with the *SCS Polaris*."

"Are you with military?"

Tony shook his head. "No . . . well, not exactly. We're with the Science Conglomerate. It works indirectly with the military."

One man, holding Charlie, said, "Scientists! They're here for us. We knew they'd come."

Another man asked, "Should we kill them?"

The woman said, "I . . . don't want . . . "

At that moment, Bill appeared with several others. Some didn't have all the metal parts and were dressed more like medical doctors than warriors.

"Wait, Esther! It's okay." An elder man in a doctor's outfit stopped her.

"Luke, these people are from Earth!"

The doctor calmly said, "I know that. But I do not believe they're here for you. They don't even know about us. Oh, dear, and you have really hurt this one. Come, help bring them back to the facility."

Esther huffed, but took her foot off Tony's chest. Several of the men who had injured Charlie were now helping him to walk with a broken leg.

Tony stood up, coughing, and then looked at the doctor. "Luke . . . Doctor Luke Haun?"

Luke smiled. "Yes. You know of me?"

"Yes. You worked with my father. Ronald Henderson."

"Don't tell me you're little Anthony?"

Tony gave a small grin. "Yes. I . . . I thought you were dead?"

"I guess many people would think that. Come on, let's get back to the settlement."

A million questions ran through Tony's mind, none of them having to do with a crashed starship or why there are humans this far out. To him, he had seen a ghost.

# CHAPTER FIVE
# HIDDEN HISTORY

"Can you get them?" Captain Ham demanded.

The comm officer shook her head as she frantically pressed the button. "Sorry, sir. Their signal just . . . died."

A young woman at the science station reported. "I read their power signature on the planet for a moment, and now it's gone."

"Did you read any sign of struggle, an explosion, anything?"

"No, Captain. It's like they vanished. I saw them landing, and then the signal slowly faded away."

Captain Ham stood up and joined the science officer at her station. "Exactly what did we read?"

She checked her sensor history for a moment. "I saw them land and then vanish from sensors just about the time that signal came through."

He looked at the readings. "No weapons fire, no sign of crash. Just a garbled distress signal."

The second officer looked up at him. "Should we send shuttle one down to investigate?"

Captain Ham returned to his seat. "No. We risk having the same thing happen to them. Procedure is clear on this situation. We are to return to Federated Space and signal for assistance from a full

Military Cruiser and that's exactly what we'll do. Helm, plot a course and take us to subspace immediately. Don't take us too far from this system. I want to be here when they come to help."

"This will take at least three days, and that's not assuming how long it will take a full cruiser to arrive." The second officer stated.

"Our hope is to follow procedure. Helm, engage."

"Understood." The Polaris turned and sped away from the planet.

Tony sat on a table inside a small examination room. There were five other tables here. Charlie lay on a table while Dr. Haun bandaged him. The woman who had held Tony down was currently checking him over.

She was dark-skinned with brilliant brown eyes. Her hair was pulled back in long locks that had natural items woven in. On her face, she sported a metal plate with a small lens where her right eye would be.

After checking him over, she said, "You seem fine. No broken ribs. Just some light bruising."

"Light . . . I'm gonna feel that kick of yours for a week."

She gave him an icy glare. "I will defend my home."

"I'm sorry, just joking. So, your name is Esther?"

She put away her tools. "Yes."

"An interesting name. Sort of old-fashioned."

She nodded back. "Dr. Luke gave it to me."

"He named you? Is he your father?"

She put the tray away. "Might as well be. Never knew my father or mother, don't remember much before they took me."

"Took?" Tony asked.

Dr. Luke came over. "It is a long story. Why don't we have something to eat, and I'll tell you all about it?"

Esther protested. "But, doctor, they can't be here when . . ."

"Don't worry. I'm sure they'll be gone soon enough. Why don't you get some recharging in before the sun sets."

"Yes, doctor."

"Recharging?" Tony asked.

"All in good time. Come, we have some very nice fruits and berries native to this world. I think you'll like them."

Dr. Luke and Tony left the medical building and walked across a well-built compound amid this lush forest. People walked around, most of them sporting the same metal plates as Esther. Both entered a large building with tables spread out. A few others were eating, all of which did not have any metal plates on their bodies.

"Here, have a bowl of sun berries—that is what we call them. They remind me of strawberries." He handed Tony a bowl of large, orange and yellow berries that looked almost painted with color.

Tony sat down and ate one. "Nice. Really sweet."

"They grow in the mild climates on this world. We farm them in the second settlement down the hill."

Tony motioned with a sun berry in his hand. "What's going on here? The last time I heard anything about you was years ago when I was a kid. Dad said you had joined a missionary team heading for Delta Sigma Colony. That colony was destroyed by the Kalshon at the end of the war, and everyone died."

"That is what the press could say." Luke looked around for a moment, making sure that no one could hear him. "I wouldn't trust just anyone with this story, but I know you're a good man because your father was a wonderful person. Yes, I went with a team of doctors to DS Colony. You know that colony was set up as a place to harbor orphans from the war."

Tony nodded. "Yeah, it was supposed to be temporary. Just a safe place for them until the conflict was over."

"We went to offer medical aid and to bring the Gospel to them. However, just before the war was over, we started noticing that some kids were going missing. Of course, we were concerned. But no one could find them, and the military at the DS colony was no help. Then, one afternoon, a girl came in, one of the missing children. She was almost dead. I went to help and found something terrible. Someone had experimented on her, implanted bio-tech to enhance her body. After running a few minor tests, I could only conclude they were working on a super-soldier program. And they were using orphans as their future army."

"That's horrible!" Tony bellowed but was shushed by Luke. "Sorry."

"The others wouldn't want me telling you about this, but I have been harboring this secret for years. I have prayed deeply that I could find someone to tell who could tell others. Maybe get us out of here."

"How did you get here? DS colony is a long way from this sector. This isn't even Federated Space."

"It is Federated Space, but only those in the know, know. The Kalshon War suddenly took a turn in our favor, and surrender was inevitable. The super-soldiers were not needed." He spent a moment trying to put this to words. "They . . . euthanized two dozen children in their attempt to cover this up. I went to them, knowing I would risk my life by letting them know I knew, but I begged for another option. By the grace of God, they listened. Only, the agreement was prison.

This world is a haven for us, but it is also our prison. We cannot leave. Once a month an automated supply ship drops cargo down for us, and that is all the contact we've had with the outside world."

"So, that's why the signal generator is sending a reading of this planet."

Luke nodded. "Yes. It's their way of keeping us hidden."

"If they were children, how come the implants are fitting full adults?"

Luke cast his eyes down in shame. "I agreed to learn how to manage their implants. Over the years I have been given the parts to upgrade as they grew. I cannot remove them. I have studied that at length. But I can help manage them so these people are healthy."

"Why did your friends attack us?" Tony asked.

"They're scared. They know what they are and worry that someone will take them away and make them kill people. They're built to be aggressive, to be violent."

"That Esther said you named her?"

Luke smiled. "Yes. The conditioning to change them caused memory loss. Most remember nothing before they were altered. That includes names. I gave them names, all from scripture, all about hope."

Tony frowned. "I have to tell someone about this. This is wrong. These people don't need to live in fear. And we need to punish the person behind this."

Luke smiled. "I love that spirit. But let me finish before you write your angry letter to the courts. The man who started and oversaw the program was General Vantis."

Tony dropped a berry back into the bowl. He stared at Luke with wide eyes. "No. William Vantis, the current President?"

"The very same."

"He won the election because he was such a noble war hero. In fact, he touted his victory over the Kalshon during the supposed battle at DS colony," Tony said.

"Now you see our dilemma. Yes, I want you to tell others, but I don't know how anything can be changed. I have left this in God's hands."

Tony let out a slow sigh. "If I'm the answer to your prayer, then you're going to be disappointed. I'm just a scientist."

Luke smiled. "Never underestimate God. Now, you and your friends can get a good night's sleep. Then it's back to your shuttle."

"That . . . might be a problem. The power died on our shuttle."

"Yup, no power near this colony. That's by design. It dampens the implants and keeps the people here thinking and being human. Those implants turn them into something ugly. But they keep some benefits, such as good strength. A team of them will carry your shuttle to the edge of the dampening zone. That should allow you to get enough energy back to fly away."

"I just hope my ship isn't too worried about us right now. We haven't been able to contact them since we landed."

"I'm sure they'll be fine."

# CHAPTER SIX
## SEARCHING

Captain Ham sat, eyebrows drawn in serious thought, yet his eyes drooped. Everyone on the bridge waited in silence as they went about their work.

"Captain, you need rest," Commander Shepard stated.

Captain Ham looked at his first officer. "I know. But I won't be able to sleep if I tried. Tony is my oldest friend. We've been through a lot together. I was the last person who ever talked to his father and promised him I would watch out for his son. I know it's unbecoming of a Captain, but I am scared."

Commander Shepard smiled. "It's okay. I know you and Tony are more friends than coworkers. But you still need sleep."

Before Captain Ham could reply to that, the Comm station announced. "Sir, we have an incoming message. It's from the . . . the . . . " She went pale. "Sir, it's from the *USS Washington*."

Goosebumps crawled over Captain Ham. "The Flagship! Put it through."

Suddenly the smiling face of a well-dressed, distinguished man appeared. "Hello, *SCS Polaris*, this is President Vantis on the *USS Washington*."

Roger stood at attention. "Mr. President, sir!"

"At ease, Captain. I'm just letting you know we got your message and are on our way to assist."

"Begging your pardon, Mr. President, but why is the Flagship of the Earth Fleet responding to this?"

Vantis flashed that million-dollar smile. "We were the closest when the call came in. Now, be ready to rendezvous at the edge of Federated Space in three days."

"Aye, sir."

Tony lay in bed, listening to the menagerie of animal and insect sounds outside his window. It was seldom he had spent this much time in a place without power. However, it also made it difficult to get to sleep.

Staring at the ceiling, wondering what that squeaking bug was outside his window, Tony finally got up. He put his shirt back on and strolled outside in the dark, cool air. He walked without direction for a moment, the sweet aroma of flowers wafting by on the chilly breezes, a milky white cloud passed by the second of this world's three moons. The deep dark skies held millions of points of light, dazzling above him.

"Mr. Tony, did you need something?" A familiar voice greeted him.

He turned and found Esther walking up. "Oh, good evening. No, I was just taking a brief walk. Can't seem to get to sleep."

"Oh. You looked like you were searching for something." She said this and took a step to leave.

"I wasn't searching, just enjoying the peace here."

"Peace?"

Tony took in a deep breath and let it out with a satisfied expression. "You probably know little about other worlds, having lived here for over twenty years. But most other Federated worlds are far more technological and busier. Places like this are rare and highly treasured. So calm, so peaceful."

"I like to imagine myself on other worlds. I look at them as often as I can," Esther quietly said.

"What do you mean?"

She hesitated for a second and then smiled. "Come, I'll show you."

Grabbing his hand, she pulled him across the compound, and up a short hill. At the top there was a little building with a dome on top.

"An observatory?" Tony asked.

Esther nodded. "Dr. Luke says this was the first thing built here, by explorers before we came. They wanted to use this world to study the far reaches of space. But they had to leave during the war and never returned. We like to come up here and look."

He walked in and was in awe. "This is a type 109b telescope, one of the most pristine ground-based telescopes. It's a bit old, but still in great shape. I would give anything to have one of these babies to play with."

"You know how to use it?"

Tony grinned. "My specialty is long-range exploration, and I'm the current field head for the Hubble project."

"Oh, show me . . . . Everything!" She had the eagerness of a child.

Tony sat with her in the two-person observation stand as they peered through the lenses. All night, they looked at distant objects as he explained the various places. Enthralled, she could not pry herself from the telescope as he showed her the universe.

"I didn't know that was the center of the galaxy." She pressed her eye into the lens.

"Few telescopes can get this kind of resolution without power."

She looked at him, that gleam of happiness in her eye. "This is so amazing."

He then said something that came out before he thought. "You have really beautiful eyes."

She coyly looked away. "What?"

"I . . . uh . . . I didn't mean. I was just. Um." He changed the subject. "Now, I want to show you my ship. This should be neat. Watching a ship in orbit has always been one of my favorite things . . . " He paused as he altered the telescope again and again. "That's strange. She's not there."

"Who?"

"The *Polaris*. The orbital path of the ship is precisely calculated. They wouldn't deviate. And they wouldn't have left the planet since we lost contact with them."

"Is this bad?"

"I don't know. Might just be me. I'm exhausted. It's been a long night."

"It's almost morning. I should get some breakfast ready. I'm on food duty this morning." She hopped down from the telescope seat.

He followed her. "It's early for breakfast?"

"Normally, yes. But today is the day Luke preaches a morning sermon. So, there is food earlier. We non-human people just absorb sunlight to fuel our systems. It's just about the only process that still works under this energy dampening shield. So, we don't need to eat."

They walked out into the early glow of the morning. "Is Luke a good preacher?"

"I guess. I stopped going to sermons a while back." She continued toward the kitchen.

"Why?"

"He has taught us our entire lives. We know everything about Jesus and the Gospel. But . . . I . . . it's hard . . . I really don't want to talk about it." She pushed the door open to the kitchen and went inside.

Tony almost followed when Charlie ran up. "Tony!"

He found both Charlie and Bill with several of the metal plated people. "What's wrong?"

Bill gestured to the others around him. "They carried the shuttle out and we got just beyond the energy dampening shields. The comm system came online, but we couldn't get a signal."

"It might not be strong enough yet. It'll take time for the solar . . ." Tony said.

"No, we got a strong signal sent. But it didn't connect. The ship isn't there."

"That means they followed standard procedure and went to find help. I guess we're stuck here for a few days."

"What do we do, sir?" Charlie asked.

"You and Bill relax; help out if you can. You stay off that leg as much as possible. I think . . . I will put my knowledge of old telescopes to use."

"Tony!" Esther called out from the door into the observatory.

Tony pulled himself out from under the telescope. "Oh, hey there. Just finishing those adjustments to the crank system. This thing is going to be so smooth."

Esther came over with a box. "I brought some lunch. But I suppose this could be breakfast. You have been here since dawn and haven't eaten."

He sat up and pulled a sandwich out of the box. "The last thing I need is a mother pestering me to eat."

"You need one. You don't take solar charges and you work yourself to death."

He took a big bite and talked right around it. "It is kinda nice to have someone worry about you. Now, did you get that lever oiled up?"

She left him and picked up the lever from the table. "Yes."

"Lemme see." He held out his hand.

She handed it to him, which nearly dropped his arm to the ground. "Oops, sorry. It's really heavy."

He laughed. "And I don't have your amazing strength." He examined it. "Good, the blacksmith did excellent work."

She took it and began the attaching process. "It's amazing what we've accomplished in just two days."

"I know. You're a fast learner."

She pushed hard to set the lever. "It's nice when the teacher is fun to listen to."

"So, you like me?" He smiled, his mouth bulging with food. Which made her laugh.

# CHAPTER SEVEN
# BROKEN CONNECTIONS

Two more days passed while Tony and the two other security guards continued helping the people fix minor issues around the camp. Almost every waking moment, Esther and Tony worked on the observatory. It was hard to find them apart from each other. She even sat with him when he ate dinner, talking up a storm about all the places he has been.

"Okay, take your seat." Tony gestured to the seat opposite his at the base of the telescope.

Esther sat down with a giddy smile.

He took his seat next to her and looked her in the eyes. "It's all yours. Crank her up."

Esther cranked the large arm, and the telescope moved into place. Then she turned a different crank, and the platform turned, moving the dome with it. The dark night sky beamed down the pale moonlight through the opening. She carefully watched the dials. "Just six . . . more . . . and there it is." She leaned over and looked through. "Beautiful."

"Let me see." He leaned over as well and shared the view. They were looking at the Terran solar system, Earth. From here, it was hardly a few dots orbiting a larger dot, but it was impressive at this distance.

"Earth. It seems like a dream, a place that doesn't really exist," she said.

Tony sat back and just gazed up through the opening. "One day, Esther, I'm going to show you all the wonderful places of Earth. My favorite are the mountains, but the Grand Canyon isn't bad either. Oh, and I . . . Esther, what's wrong?"

Tears fell from her one real eye. "It's . . . nothing."

"I'm sorry. I shouldn't have talked about Earth like that."

"No. It's not that. It's you."

He frowned. "Me? Did I do something wrong?"

"No. I just . . . I never thought I would like someone how I like you."

His frown faded into almost a smile. "I like you too, Esther."

"No, you can't. I'm not real. No one can love me. I . . . I . . . " She turned and ran out of the Observatory.

"Esther, wait!" He followed quickly.

She hadn't gone far. Standing outside in the chilly night air, her face was buried deep in her hands. "Please, don't." She wept.

He put his hands on her shoulders. "Esther. Why do you believe this? It isn't true. You can be loved, just like anyone. And you're real."

"No. I'm just a machine. They stole my humanity when I was a child. They made me into this abomination."

"They altered you, yes. But you're still human. Love is one of the greatest things, Jesus said so. He died for us because of love. We live for Him and for each other because of love. Can't you see that?"

She turned on him, slapping his hands away. "Don't you understand! Without the energy dampening field, I would become mindless. I would kill you. I would be at the whim of whoever controlled me. That's not human! This is why I know God can't save me, I can't have salvation, Jesus didn't die for robots, for killing machines."

Tony grabbed her by the hand. "He died for your soul! You have a soul. I know it! I see it when you look at the stars, I see it when you work with passion, I see it in your smile. Yes, I can like you, even love you, and God's love is infinitely greater than mine."

She looked up, those tears quivering on her cheeks. "I wish I could believe that." With that, she fled down the hill, running away from him.

Captain Ham sat at the command of the *Polaris* while they entered orbit. Next to them was the much larger *USS Washington*.

"Sir, what do we do now?" Commander Shepard asked.

Captain Ham shook his head. "I don't know. At this point the president will call the shots. Comm, see if you can . . . "

Just then the screen came on with the president smiling at them. "Ah, good. We're going to enter the atmosphere to deal with this situation. I want you to stay in orbit. Wait for further instruction." The screen cut back to space.

Captain Ham and Commander Shepard both looked at each other in confusion.

"Sir, the *Washington* is heading through the atmosphere."

"Hold our position."

Tony walked through the compound in the early morning sunlight. He searched for Esther but couldn't find her. He saw Luke heading for the kitchen and followed.

"Luke!" He ran inside.

"Morning, Tony. I thought I'd see you. Come, get something to eat with me."

Tony picked up a bowl of an oatmeal-like mush with butter on it. "Why did you expect me?"

"I was paid a late visit by Esther last night. She wasn't feeling well."

Tony sat down across from Luke. "Look, I'm sorry. I didn't mean to cause her to get all emotional. I guess I missed all the signs we were clicking. I don't have a lot of experience with girls."

Luke stirred the butter into his oatmeal. "She wasn't upset with you. She was questioning herself. You have inspired something in her I've failed to do in twenty years as her pastor. She understands what it means to be loved."

"But we hardly know each other."

"You two know each other better than you believe. But it is true that this is merely a budding relationship. However, it is foreign to her. She has fought with the teachings of the scriptures her entire life. She convinced herself years ago that she was nothing more than some kind of machine, unworthy of love or salvation. We're like family here, but she never connected with anyone on that deeper level until you. You brought out in her feelings that are hard but good for her. I hope it's the start of something."

"I just hate that she isn't feeling well. She was so happy and then this."

Luke smiled. "Spoken like a person in love. You worry about her feelings first. That shows me she might have done something special to you."

All at once the sunlight beaming through the windows was snuffed by a great shadow. A rumbling engine rattled the walls and people screamed outside.

"What's going on?" Luke stood up.

A buzzing sound interrupted them. Tony noticed an old monitor implanted into the wall. "What's that?"

Luke looked back at the wall. "It's part of the original building. It shouldn't be working."

Just then President Vantis appeared, smiling at them. "Refugee compound. I'm afraid that your time's up."

Luke looked back at the doors when the screaming became shrill, as if deadly animals were outside.

The President continued. "This noble experiment has ended. I cannot risk this being known and so I'll deal with it as I should have twenty-five years ago. I'm so sorry for this but know your sacrifices will only improve our society."

Tony held up his arm and saw his wrist comm blinking. "Oh, no. This can't be good. The power dampening field is no longer working. My device is active."

"No!" Luke ran for the door. "The implanted people, they'll be activated."

Just as he opened the door, the body of one of his regular workers crashed through a window and was sent flying over several tables. The bloody remains of this man rested in a pile of debris.

"Get in here! Now!" Luke waved madly.

Tony looked out and gasped to see dozens of those metal implanted people walking toward them in a zombie-like state. They shoved over trees and smashed objects as they marched to kill. The non-implanted people raced toward safety. Charlie hobbled along with his leg still in a cast, Bill helping him move. They both were going too slow.

"Charlie!" Tony ran out to help his friend when he noticed two of the implanted people almost on them. They stopped and jerked, flinching and straining. Then more of them fought this. They cried out, screamed, called out to God. In this state of confusion, Tony got his friends inside.

Luke frowned. "What's going on?"

"I don't know. But I doubt this is part of their programming."

Workers raced inside, filling this place. Some carried anything they could that would be useful as a weapon. It would do little good against these enhanced people, but it was a desperate time. Two bolstered the doors with a make-shift blockade.

Just then the blockade burst apart as the super-soldiers crawled through. To his horror, the first person was Esther. She stumbled as she walked, her motions jerky and forced.

"Is that normal for them to walk like zombies?" Tony asked.

Luke shook his head. "No. They're designed for precision movement."

"H . . . he . . . help!" she cried out.

Tony went for her, but Bill held him back. "No, sir, she'll kill you."

Tony shook his head. "I don't care. I have to try. She doesn't deserve this." He ran over just as she fell to her knees. "Esther, are you in there?"

She held him by the arms, her grip almost breaking his bones. "Please . . . I . . . I don't want to . . . kill."

"Watch it!" Bill swung a large piece of wood and hit a different implanted person in the face just as he was about to attack Tony.

Esther cried, tears streaming down her face. "I . . . won't kill. Please . . . God . . . show mercy . . . Take me first . . . I don't want to kill."

Tony pulled her closer. "Let him take over. It is the only way. Surrender to him."

She wailed. "I want to be human! I want to love! I want Jesus to love me! I accept His love!" Then she slumped over his shoulder.

Suddenly another man yelled. "Jesus, save me!"

Another cried out. "Stop me, Lord!"

As they spoke, they would crumple to the ground and stop their onslaught.

Luke gently knelt next to Tony and put a hand on Esther's shoulder. "Do you surrender to Him?"

She shook with tears as she said, "I surrender all that I am. I don't want anyone else controlling my life."

Tony slowly lifted her from him and looked into her wet face. "I'm so proud of you."

"Can you love me too?" She whispered.

"I can certainly try."

"We have to help them. They're in pain." Luke waved at his assistants to join him.

Tony handed her off to Luke and stood. "Are they going to be all right?"

Luke shook his head. "I don't know. I will try."

Tony watched as the aids and Luke took the people away. The whole time he formulated an idea. With a quick motion, he typed into his comm device.

After a long conversation, and a lot of cleaning up by the people, Tony waited for what would come next. He lifted his arm and typed in the command. The screen opened to the bridge of the *Washington*.

"What is the meaning of this?" President Vantis demanded.

Tony smiled with Luke at one side and Esther on his other. "Mr. President, your game of death is over."

"I don't understand. Soldier, why are you not doing your duty?" He glared at Esther.

"Go to—"

Luke stopped Tony with a shushing shake of his head.

Luke smiled at the President. "Looks like your people taught me too well. I have worked for decades to remove the horrid programming. I didn't think I succeeded, but all I needed was for a full activation. Their emotional state overwhelmed the programming and shorted out the control chips in their brains."

"What is this gibberish? That technology is beyond you. This is not possible. Soldier, I order you to finish your duty!"

Tony glared. "Sir, you'll find there are authorities in this universe far greater than yours. If I were you, I'd be more concerned about the Judicial Court."

"What about the Court?"

"Yes, if you check your sensors, the *SCS Polaris* just left the system. It's a Class Seven explorer vessel, with top-of-the-line engines. Much faster than the *Washington*. They'll reach communication range with the Court sooner than you. I have just transmitted all the data pertaining to your little super-soldier experiment, including a statement by Dr. Luke Haun, and three statements by three of your experiments. All of which demonstrate you broke several intergalactic laws in this failed program. *And* you attempted to commit genocide to cover your tracks but were forced to wrongfully imprison people in a secret penal colony. I'm sure when the Court finds out about all of this, your time in office will be through and you'll be facing jail time."

President Vantis stood from his seat. "How dare you threaten me!"

"Threaten, no, just telling you what is going to happen."

The President glared at them. "What gives you the right to act like this to your president?"

Luke quoted Scripture. *"'But if anyone causes one of these little ones who believe in Me to stumble, it would be better for him to have a large millstone hung around his neck and to be thrown into the sea.'* Mr. President, you turned children into murderers. There are no depths of the sea fit for the crimes you have committed."

The President yelled, "All weapons, fire at that colony!"

"Sir . . . that's a human colony?" the man beside him said.

"I said fire!"

There was a quiet moment, and then a soldier took the president by the arm. "Sir, I think you need to be relieved of command of this vessel. Please escort the president . . . " The comm line cut off.

In moments, the shadow over the compound moved off, returning the wash of sunlight across the land.

# CHAPTER EIGHT
# INTO THE UNKNOWN

**Two weeks later.**

Esther stood with Tony on the observation deck of the Polaris. They flew next to the same nebula they had first placed the HRN14. The colors dancing in the clouds bathed them both in glorious light. She leaned up against him, cuddling his arm.

"I can't believe I'm really here," she cooed.

He held her hand. "To be honest, I feel the same way. I think we both are experiencing life anew."

"Sir?" 865 walked up.

"Is it time?" Tony asked.

"Yes, sir. The judge is waiting to speak with you personally."

Tony led Esther down the corridor. "A month ago, I thought planting a new satellite would be my biggest achievement. Now, I'm part of the trial of the century against the President. How God leads us to places we never expect, He takes us into the unknown."

*They are on the trail of a rogue cleric. Yet PFC Kalen Richardson wonders how he could be any help in a team of battle-hardened soldiers heading to a jungle planet. His answer comes in a surprising twist of fate.*

# ROOKIE
## ERIC LANDFRIED

# CHAPTER ONE
# FIRST CLASS KALEN

Private First Class Kalen Richardson's stomach lurched as the jumpship roughly punched its way through the planet's atmosphere, emerging from the cold darkness of the null into a land of lush, tropical greenery. Kalen swallowed hard, tightly gripping the barrel of the cluster rifle in front of him, willing himself not to vomit, because he knew if he did, the veteran troopers in his unit would never let him live it down. His sharpshooting skills may have bought him a place on the squad, but he knew it would take time and strong, selfless effort to endear himself to the other members.

He glanced out the porthole just over his shoulder, noting a rich, lavender sky dotted with wisps of clouds. As someone who grew up on a planet consisting mostly of noisy cities and pollution-belching factories, Kalen stared in awe at this new environment. It looked like a paradise.

A short, but loud whistle took his attention away from the porthole and brought it over to his unit commander, Captain Peabody. The captain wasn't an overly large man, but he radiated a large presence. The burn scars on his face and hands alone proved his toughness and mettle as a soldier, so Kalen already had the highest level of respect for him. Peabody stepped away from the cockpit door from which he'd just emerged and stalked slowly between the troopers seated on either side of the jumpship's aisle.

"All right, boys, listen up. Cleric Scott has some words and intel for you, so you *will* pay him your full attention. And if I see you're not, I *will* chew you up and spit you out like spoiled leftovers. Am I clear?"

The answer came quickly from the entire unit, "Sir! Yes, sir!"

The cockpit door opened, and Cleric Dawson Scott stepped out, sweeping his robes around himself so they wouldn't be caught in the closing door. Kalen had never seen a cleric in the flesh before, so he looked on intently, studying every detail of the man's features and clothing. Like every cleric, he was dressed in the traditional burgundy robe trimmed with gold piping around the edges. As he walked forward, the front of the robe opened slightly, and Kalen saw he was wearing a white linen shirt and pants with an off-white sash around his waist. Instead of the traditional sandals, he wore knee-high boots, no doubt to deal with the expected rough terrain on the planet below. Cleric Scott strode forward, locking his crystal blue eyes onto each trooper. His long handsome face had sharp features crowned with neatly coiffed blond hair, and when he smiled Kalen noticed his teeth were perfectly straight and sparkling white.

"Good afternoon, gentlemen," Cleric Scott began, "you should all feel proud, for you have been chosen for a mission of utmost importance. As you know, clerics such as myself are responsible for meting out justice in our society. We are *very* important men and women with a *very* important job. If a society has no justice, then all we have is chaos, a free-for-all, a battle royale where only the strong survive, and the weak who *do* survive are trampled down in oppression.

"It is because of this possibility that I take my position so very seriously, as I believe every cleric should. But of course, each of us clerics are human, susceptible to selfish desires and the temptations that can be found in any society. It is always important that justice should thrive, that the guilty should be punished, but when a cleric falls to the level of a common criminal, it is doubly important that justice be served.

"I volunteered for this mission because I believe these things with my whole heart. Gentlemen, I am grieved to announce this, but our quarry is my former brother, Alger Mander."

A gasping murmur rippled through the squad. Kalen instantly recognized the name from the news. Alger Mander, the rogue cleric, a zealot who had lost his mind chasing a fugitive, slaughtering a squad of troopers and setting off a starburst bomb that killed thousands of men, women, and children. Mander had disappeared without a trace, so it surprised Kalen that he had finally been tracked down.

As Cleric Scott waited for the whispers to subside, Captain Peabody barked at the squad, "Pipe down, boys, the cleric's not done talking!"

The troopers obeyed and Cleric Scott gave a small nod to the captain before he continued. "I'm glad to see you all understand the gravity and importance of this mission. After all, the arbiters of justice must obey the law as well as uphold it, or the people will *never* trust the office of the clerics again. Cleric Mander *must* pay for his atrocities, and that's why I asked for the best of the best to help me bring him to justice. I've spent the last five years tracking this monster down, and of course, I found him on a non-Federation planet. As I investigated him, I realized it made perfect sense for him to shun the very society he once upheld. After searching several non-Federation planets, I found the evidence I was looking for. He's here, gentlemen, down there in that jungle. My research shows there are lifeforms on the planet, mostly animal, but some humanoid as well. Considering the lack of civilization, my best guess is that these humanoids are indigenous tribes who may be able to help us in finding Mander.

"Your captain will give you orders on how to proceed once we land but be forewarned. This planet is very beautiful, but it may also be very deadly. We may be facing animals and/or people who could react to our presence with hostility, and you should all be prepared for that possibility. Do not be afraid to defend yourself. In addition to that, you should keep in mind that Mander is a crafty, devious man. Watch out for booby traps and watch out for him, for he is a highly skilled warrior and will have no qualms about taking your life. Lastly, I thank you all for coming with me in this most historic moment. Mander is the first rogue cleric we have ever had in the history of the Federation, and I believe that our success in this mission will prove that he will always be the last."

Cleric Scott turned, swirling his robes with a haughty flourish, and strode back toward the cockpit. Captain Peabody rose, ready to call for a gear check before they landed. And then, as the cockpit door closed behind Cleric Scott, the jumpship's right engine exploded.

# CHAPTER TWO
# BEYOND THE RIVER

Wind blasting into his face awoke Kalen, and he opened his eyes to see the treetops rushing headlong at him. With a cry of alarm, his hands scrambled across his chest, searching desperately for the ripcord to his parachute. He felt the loop with his left hand and hooked a finger through it, giving a terrified yank. The chute began to deploy, and Kalen prayed frantically that it would go faster, that the Lord would somehow speed up the process before he slammed into the ground. Just before he reached the leafy treetops, the chute opened, and the harness pulled taut. Kalen breathed a sigh of relief as the wind caught the chute and slowed his descent. However, the trees proved thick and heavy with vegetation, and they grabbed and snagged the parachute, leaving Kalen suspended fifty feet from the ground. Once his descent had stopped, Kalen breathed a sigh of exasperation and tried to remember where to find the release strap for the chute. As he searched, something hissed to his right, and he looked up into the eyes of a small squirrel-like creature, its brown fur dappled with orange spots that helped it blend against the trunks of the trees. The creature's small round head observed Kalen for a second, then it hissed again, its open mouth revealing sharp fangs and a forked tongue. Startled, Kalen cried out and fumbled at his waist for his sidearm, but by the time he'd freed it from its holster, the creature had vanished.

*Probably more scared of me than I am of it.*

He attempted to holster his sidearm, but somehow missed the pocket, and the weapon fell from his grasp, clattering against branches as it dropped to the ground. Kalen rolled his eyes at his clumsiness, then found the chute's release strap a few seconds later. Once free of the parachute harness, he carefully climbed down out of the trees, grateful to finally have both his boots on the ground.

He looked around briefly for any other members of his squad but saw no one. The jungle canopy proved too thick to see much of anything beyond it except a few spots where the leaves had parted enough to let pinholes of sunlight through, so Kalen had no way of determining which way was north.

*So much for the old-fashioned way.* He lifted his left forearm and tapped a few buttons on his electronic gauntlet. Seconds later, the gauntlet sent out a blue light in all directions as it scanned the terrain for a mile radius, reporting back with a crude map of the area. Kalen noticed the presence of a river and decided to head there, figuring there might be enough open sky by the water to determine his next move. As he had been trained, he checked his gear first, but when he went to pick up his fallen sidearm, it was nowhere to be found. Filled with annoyed surprise, Kalen searched all around the tree as well as some of the surrounding trees. His cluster rifle had obviously fallen from his hands while he was unconscious, and now the loss of his sidearm left him completely unarmed. Not wanting to waste any more time, especially since he didn't know how long the sunlight would last, he threw up his hands in frustration and began his trek to the river.

As he turned and walked away, he completely missed the figure sitting on a branch just above him, a humanoid with ruddy skin who watched him with eyes gleaming like emeralds. The squirrel-like creature crawled up onto the figure's shoulder, chirping once, and the figure reached into the pouch at his side, past Kalen's sidearm, and brought out a handful of grain. The creature snatched a few of the kernels in its tiny paws and gobbled them greedily.

The river turned out to be a lazy stream, maybe fifty meters across. As Kalen stood on its banks, he spotted a large chunk of shrapnel from the shattered jumpship embedded in the mud on the other side. A body floated by facedown on the water, trailing a parachute, half a dozen arrows buried in its back, and Kalen was suddenly very sorry he hadn't spent more time trying to find his sidearm. He scanned the trees on both sides of the river but didn't see anyone or anything that might fire arrows at him.

Beyond the river, a column of black smoke spiraled into the sky, and Kalen assumed it came from the wreckage of the jumpship as he plunged into the river, shocked at first by the icy cold water. Shivering as he swam, he crawled up onto the opposite bank and sat for a moment, clutching his knees to his chest, letting the jungle sun warm him. Once his teeth ceased chattering, he rose and hiked a little further until he reached the smoking remnants of the jumpship.

The ship had split the jungle when it crashed, splintering trees, crushing undergrowth, and carving a trench into the earth as it skidded to a stop. Kalen surveyed the scene, wishing he'd be able to scrub the sight from his memories afterward. The ruined jumpship still smoldered, but the worst sight was the bodies strewn across the crash site. His fellow troopers, men he'd trained with and respected, lay dead before him, some of them burned beyond recognition. He desperately wanted to look away, but he forced himself to look and count each body, coming up with a total that was four short of the number of men who'd been on the ship.

Kalen knew he should try to find the three others, but he felt unsure how to even begin searching on a planet that was completely covered in jungle. Just as he steeled himself to search around the wreckage and the bodies for supplies, a voice called out from the trees, "Richardson?"

Kalen spun in his tracks, instinctively reaching for his sidearm, chiding himself for being too lazy to find it when his hand closed on emptiness. As he looked on, some of the jungle's undergrowth parted, and Captain Peabody, bruised and bloodied, crawled into the open. Kalen's eyes widened with surprise and relief as he rushed to the captain's side.

"Sir! I'm so glad to see you!"

"Same here, Private. Glad to see someone else made it out."

"I did a count, sir. It seems four of us survived. Any ideas on how to find the others?"

"If they're not wounded, they'll find their way here, like you did. We should wait here a little while longer, see if anyone else shows up."

"Sir, you should know there are natives in the area. We had five survivors, but they killed one man while he was parachuting. I saw his body in the river."

"I figured that. It's why I was hiding in the jungle. Did you see Cleric Scott among the bodies?"

"No, sir, but some of them are burned beyond recognition, so I can't be certain he isn't one of them."

"He was in the cockpit when we were hit. If you don't see him here, then I think it's safe to assume he's one of our survivors."

The captain winced as he adjusted his sitting position, and a small grunt of pain escaped his lips.

"What's wrong, sir?" Kalen asked.

"Broken leg, Private," the captain answered, "If we do end up searching for the others, you'll have to do all the searching."

"Not a problem, sir. I won't let you down."

"I appreciate the eagerness, Private, but first maybe find me something I can use to splint this leg?"

Before Kalen could answer, a high-pitched voice said something in a burbling, alien language, and they both looked up at a humanoid with dark orange skin, large, sparkling green eyes, and a shock of wiry brown hair that stuck out in all directions. It was dressed in a simple beige tunic that came down to just above its knobby knees, and Kalen noticed its large, bare feet with long, simian-like toes. But the worst for Kalen was that the creature was holding his sidearm and pointing it at them.

When the captain saw the weapon, he glanced at Kalen's empty holster and said, "Well, private, if we survive this, expect some discipline for losing your weapon when we get home."

Kalen lowered his head dejectedly. "Yes, sir."

# CHAPTER THREE
# THE NATIVES

Kalen dropped in exhaustion to his knees and carefully lowered Captain Peabody, who he'd just carried three kilometers through the jungle, to the ground. The native behind them lowered Kalen's sidearm and then shouted a high-pitched, ululating call at the small cluster of huts before them. Seconds later, the call was returned in dozens of voices as more natives poured out of the huts, and a crowd of curious onlookers quickly grew in front of them. A smaller native, likely a child, stepped forward and ran its long fingers through Kalen's red hair, burbling something that Kalen thought sounded like a question.

"Uh, yeah, that's my hair," Kalen explained.

The native child said something he didn't understand, but before he could make any response, a larger native scooped up the child and pulled it back into the crowd, chirping at it in a scolding tone. Kalen looked at Captain Peabody.

"What should we do, sir?"

"Not sure just yet, Private. We were marched here at the end of a gun, but these people don't strike me as overly violent. They seem somewhat . . . domesticated."

A tinny trumpet blast drew their attention to the largest of the huts. The native who'd blown the trumpet let his sour note hang in the air for a second before he knelt by the hut's door. Another native, larger than most of the others, emerged from the hut, dressed in the most regal finery the jungle could offer. His face was framed in red and white feathers jutting out in a circle, and he wore a tunic striped in vibrant colors rather than the plain beige all the others wore.

"Well, I think we know who's in charge, now," said the captain.

As the colorfully dressed native walked forward, all the other natives knelt and bowed their heads in deference. Once he stood before Kalen and Peabody, he glared at them with a haughty eye and spoke something that sounded ominous despite the high pitch of his voice.

"I don't understand a word these creatures say," said the captain, "but I'm not sure I like this one's tone."

The native leader, apparently incensed at the captain speaking, shouted angrily and marched over to the native who still held Kalen's firearm. He snatched the pistol and pointed it at the captain, still burbling away in his language.

The captain lowered his head, ready to accept his fate, but everything stopped when a voice called out, "Ho! Please stay your hand, mighty chieftain!"

All eyes shifted toward the larger hut as a man emerged, his ebony skin shining in the sun. A tall, black afro and a bushy beard streaked with gray surrounded his face. He flashed a smile of perfect, stark white teeth as he approached and called, "Welcome to Qatixi, Captain Peabody! It's good to see you again!"

Kalen looked at the captain. "Sir, is that who I think it is?"

"Well, Private, if you think that's Alger Mander, then yes, you'd be correct."

"You keep the sidearm, Private. You were the best shot before we crashed and definitely the best shot now. It will be better in your hands than mine if we need it."

"Yes, Captain."

Kalen secured his newly returned sidearm in its holster and watched as a native medicine man carefully splinted Captain Peabody's broken leg. He looked surprised when a bowl of warm food was pressed into his hands at Alger Mander's orders. Only now realizing just how hungry he was, he scooped a bit of the yellowish mush from the bowl into his mouth, and his eyebrows raised at the flavor of sweet, fruity deliciousness. All the while, he watched as Mander spoke English to the natives, which they clearly understood, and then listened to their replies in their language, which Mander seemed to understand as well. As he watched Mander at work, he couldn't help but think that this man didn't seem like some kind of mass-murdering demon.

After checking the medicine man's work on the captain's leg, Mander approached Kalen and smiled broadly.

"Ah, they fed you. Very good. The food is good, is it not?"

Kalen nodded as he swallowed another mouthful. "What is it?"

"The staple of their diet, a special fruit that only grows here. I call it blissfruit since I can't pronounce it in their language."

"How do you understand them without speaking their language?"

Mander smiled. "That was quite the chore when I first landed here. What I've learned is that the Qatixi people have a different anatomy than we do when it comes to their vocal cords. They are incapable of speaking anything other than their own language, and we can't speak theirs. I worked very hard with them, memorizing the sounds they make while they did the same for me, and now we understand each other. Which makes it very easy to proclaim the Lord's Truth to them."

"You're . . . you're here as a missionary?"

"But of course! The Qatixi need the Lord like everyone else. Why wouldn't I be here?"

"But what about—"

Kalen stopped himself, not sure he wanted to confront Mander directly with an accusation.

"About what? The fact that I'm a rogue cleric? That I'm accused of murdering civilians and soldiers?"

His words hung in the air conspicuously, as Kalen had no response other than to stare uncomfortably at Mander. Fortunately, Mander continued the conversation, ending the awkward silence.

"Yes, I came here to escape the charges that were filed against me, but that doesn't mean I stop preaching the Lord's Truth. I *am* a cleric, after all. And besides, there's, much more to the story of my alleged crimes than you and the captain know." Mander reached out and squeezed Kalen's shoulder. "Enjoy your food, Private. There's plenty more if you're still hungry."

Mander turned with a flourish and walked back toward the captain who now rested with his leg elevated. He sat down next to the captain who looked uneasily at Mander, but they were far enough away that Kalen couldn't quite make out what they were saying. He scooped more blissfruit into his mouth and wondered about the "much more" to Mander's story.

# CHAPTER FOUR
## CLERIC MANDER

"Sir, do you think it's possible we have the wrong man?"

"Why do you think that, private?"

"Well, it's just . . . he's treated us so well. Feeding us, sheltering us, fixing your leg . . . maybe he's not who we think he is. He's even been teaching the Lord's Truth to these people."

"Did you forget the body of Sergeant Henderson? Filled with arrows by one of these natives? They attacked him without provocation while he was hanging in the air, a cowardly act, if you ask me. And *someone* blew our jumpship out of the sky. Mander has obviously trained these people to do his dirty work, and if you trust him, then you're simply a rookie fool."

The captain's words stung Kalen's ego, but he had to acknowledge their truth. These questions needed answers, and he determined to ask Mander about them in the morning. In the meantime, his weary body called for rest, so he rolled onto his side and slipped into a deep sleep just a few seconds later.

The door to Alger Mander's hut was made out of thick, giant leaves stretched over a wooden frame, so Kalen tapped very lightly, worried he would punch a hole in the leaves.

"All are welcome in my home," Mander's rich, deep voice called from inside, "Please enter!"

Kalen gently pushed the door open and entered to find Mander seated, legs crossed as he scooped his breakfast into his mouth.

"Oh, I'm sorry," said Kalen, "I didn't mean to interrupt your meal."

"Nonsense! Come in, Private! How can I help you?"

With a slight shrug, Kalen continued inside and sat on a small stool across from Mander. "I guess I have some questions."

"Well, ask them, my friend. We'll see if I have some answers."

"Well, on my way to our crash site, I saw a body in the river. He was one of ours, and it looked like he'd been shot out of the sky while he was parachuting."

"Hmm. And what did they shoot him with?"

"Uh, arrows. Half a dozen or so."

"I see. And you're wondering if I or the Qatixi had something to do with that."

"Well, yeah, and there's also the fact that someone blasted our jumpship out of the sky."

"I understand why you have these questions, Private, especially considering my reputation. All I can do is insist on the innocence of myself and the Qatixi in this situation. We have no weapons here capable of destroying a jumpship, and arrows are not something the Qatixi use. In fact, the Qatixi are quite pacifistic. I have been teaching them over the years that under certain circumstances, it is appropriate and even necessary to defend oneself."

"But if you didn't do it, then who did?"

"I have the same question, and I suspect that the answer will be revealed to us shortly. In the meantime, there's no reason to neglect your self-care. You need to eat, Private. Please help yourself to all we have."

Kalen nodded and turned toward the door, but paused, a question lingering in his mind that he wasn't sure he should ask. Mander easily read his body language and said, "Do you have something else, Private?"

After a heavy sigh, Kalen said, "I don't know why I'm here."

Mander smiled, and with a gentle tone, said, "Because the Lord wills it."

"But why me? There were better, more seasoned men than me on that ship. Now, they're all dead and I'm still alive. I'm just a useless rookie, a noob. Why does the Lord want me here?"

"Our purposes are rarely clear until after those purposes have been served. I believe the Lord makes it that way so we will learn to trust Him. He will reveal His purpose for you in time, my friend. In the meantime, *trust* Him, for He is *good*."

Kalen nodded and offered a grim smile before he left the hut. His questions had been answered, but the answers had only created more questions. He decided to keep Mander's denial from the captain until he knew more. Stewing on the subject of the Lord's purpose for his survival, he headed to the center of the village, drawn by the smell of cooking food, guided by his empty stomach.

**M**id-afternoon came, and the jungle parted as Cleric Dawson Scott emerged from the thick foliage, carrying the lifeless body of a trooper on his shoulder. Alger Mander greeted him with a beaming smile and open arms.

"Ah, Brother Dawson! You have finally decided to join us!"

Cleric Scott glared at Mander for a few seconds before answering. "We are no longer brothers, Alger. You were purged from our order after your crimes. I should kill you where you stand."

"I am sure you want to, my friend, but that would not meet the clerics' standard of justice, would it?"

Cleric Scott looked around the village at the people, his eyes resting for a second on Kalen and Captain Peabody. Kalen sensed that their presence was affecting Scott's answer.

"No, Alger, it would not. Shall we set up a tribunal?"

"Of course. But first, let us help you with your deceased friend. There is no need to carry him anymore. And I'm certain you are famished. Come, eat and rest, my brother who is no longer my brother."

A cold, steely silence settled over the village as Cleric Scott crossed the congregational area and placed the dead soldier's body near Captain Peabody and Kalen. The captain sniffed once as he examined the body and said, "Corporal Higgins, a good man and good soldier. His wife will be devastated. How did he die, Cleric Scott?"

"I found his body a few miles from the crash site. I assume he fell, didn't get his chute open in time."

The captain looked away, shaking his head. "A travesty. The whole thing is a travesty."

"Indeed, Captain," said Cleric Scott, glancing over to Kalen, "I'm glad to see one of your men made it out alive. What's your name, Private?"

Kalen got to his feet and saluted the cleric. "Private First Class Kalen Richardson, sir."

"Good to see you alive."

Mander interrupted them by pushing a bowl of steaming blissfruit into Cleric Scott's hands. "Eat, my friend! You must be famished after a day and night in the jungle!"

Cleric Scott eyed the food suspiciously. "How do I know this isn't poisoned?"

Mander shrugged. "You don't. But you know me."

The cleric held the bowl out to Kalen and said, "Taste this, Private."

Surprise and anxiety crossed Kalen's face at the request, and he said, "Sir, wouldn't it be more convincing if Mander tasted it?"

"Maybe, but I'm not eating after that scum. Now taste it, Private. That's an order."

Kalen's eyes drifted to Mander who gave him a reassuring wink. As Kalen's anxiety evaporated, he scooped some of the food into his mouth and swallowed. Cleric Scott watched him as he sat back down next to the captain, and after a few tense moments passed, the cleric shrugged and sat down to eat.

Mander clasped his hands and rubbed them together. "Now, while you eat, I will set up a tribunal. I'm looking forward to my judgment!"

Cleric Scott, looking confused and skeptical, watched Mander turn and walk away. "This jungle has stolen his mind," he said.

# CHAPTER FIVE
# DISCOVERED PURPOSE

Once Mander had the tribunal prepared, the curious Qatixi people gathered around the scene in a large semi-circle. Kalen and Captain Peabody sat on the ground with the natives. Two makeshift chairs, built from tree branches and tightly woven with shredded strips of leaves, sat facing each other in the place of attention, and Cleric Scott took the one on the left as he looked for Mander to take the right one.

"Where is he?" he growled impatiently.

"I am right here, brother," Mander called as he walked up, holding two cups that both sent wisps of steam into the air, "I have brought us something to drink."

Cleric Scott scowled. "Why would I want a hot beverage in the jungle? You're ridiculous if you think I'm drinking that."

"Come now, brother, I am only trying to be a most excellent host to you. Please do not refuse my hospitality."

As Mander tossed back his own drink, Cleric Scott rolled his eyes. "Fine, but the private will test mine first."

With a shrug, Kalen rose and took the cup from Mander. At the first sip, he shuddered as the noxious flavor washed over his tongue.

He handed the cup back to Mander and returned to his seat. Cleric Scott waited another minute and watched Kalen before finally taking the cup from Mander. He attempted to take a long drink just as Mander had done but spluttered and coughed at the terrible flavor.

"Ugh!" he cried out, "Did you brew this through a dirty sock? It's disgusting."

"Yes, it is *very* disgusting, but this is a special beverage, a tea made from leaves of what I like to call the *tryggo* plant." He glanced toward Kalen and the captain. "I called it that because *tryggo* is the Norse word for 'truth.' I thought it sounded appropriately exotic for a jungle herb. The Qatixi introduced me to its properties soon after I landed here. The man who drinks this will be compelled to tell the truth no matter what."

"But why give it to me?" cried Cleric Scott. "You as the accused are the only person who needs a drink like that."

"While your logic is impeccable, brother, you and anyone else should also be willing to drink it if you have nothing to hide."

"Well, enough of this silliness," said Cleric Scott, looking mildly nervous. "Sit down. Let's get this started."

Mander took his chair and set his cup of tea on the ground beside him. Cleric Scott dumped the rest of his tea on the ground before setting his cup down. A curious murmur rippled through the Qatixi, but the cleric paid no attention to it.

After clearing his throat, Cleric Scott said in a loud, clear voice, "Alger Mander, you have been charged with the capital crimes of murder and terrorism. How do you plead?"

"Of course, I plead not guilty."

"And who is here to aid in your defense?"

"Well, I will be defending myself, but certainly *you* can aid me in that process."

Cleric Scott broke from his procedural tone and glared at Mander. "I'm conducting the tribunal, you idiot. How could I help you with your defense?"

Mander flashed a mischievous smile, looking like a predator that had cornered his prey. "By admitting you are not here to judge my crimes but to kill me as the only witness to *your* crimes. You were there that day, were you not? You brought the starburst bomb into the city plaza, correct?"

Outraged, Cleric Scott leaped to his feet. "I did no such thing!" he shouted, but as he heard the words escape his lips, a confused look crossed his face.

Mander's mischievous grin spread even wider. "What's the matter, my friend? Are you thrown by the fact that you just spoke a lie?"

Shaken, Cleric Scott looked at Mander, then at the puddle of tea by his chair. "So . . . it doesn't force you to tell the truth?"

"What am I? An alchemist? Of course not! But in a way, it has done exactly what I said. The tea has exposed the truth, and I have Private Richardson and Captain Peabody as witnesses."

"But I haven't confessed to anything!"

"A confession won't be necessary once I file my report," called Captain Peabody. "I've seen with my own eyes what a devious, evil man you are. You pinned your own atrocities on your innocent brother. You are not worthy to wear the robes of a cleric."

Mander stood up and placed a hand on Scott's shoulder. "Tell the story, Dawson. Tell our audience how you sacrificed a squad of soldiers to capture a fugitive."

Caught in his web of deceit, Scott shook his head, resigning himself to the fact he'd been exposed. "He would have escaped if I hadn't leveled that building! He was a murderer!"

"And now, my friend, so are you. And the starburst in the plaza? Tell them why."

Scott looked at the ground. "He escaped. After he knocked you out, he ran. I chased him into the plaza, but the crowds were so thick, I lost sight of him." Scott's breathing became heavy and emotional. Kalen could see the anger rising in his face. "All those people, just walking and running through their mundane, repetitive lives. They cost me my quarry! They cost me esteem as a cleric! They cost me my reputation!"

"And so they had to pay," Mander said quietly. He let his hand slip from Scott's shoulder and turned away. "And once you found me, you brought more soldiers, intent on sacrificing them to further damage my own reputation, correct?"

Scott sighed and gave a slight nod. "I planted a charge on the jumpship's engine before we took off."

"And you assumed the natives here would be violent people, so you murdered any survivors you found with arrows, thinking the Qatixi would be blamed?" The natives hissed at Scott over this allegation, and Scott crossed his arms, seething at being further exposed as well as outsmarted by Mander.

"Yes. Yes, that was my plan."

"I am sad that your narcissism has a body count, my friend. I am truly sad that you do not have the Lord's Truth in your heart. You are a pretender, and always have been."

Scott stared at Mander his eyes wide with hatred. "You've taken everything from me," he said.

Mander looked back at him, "You don't even understand you had nothing to begin with."

With a roar of rage, Scott lunged at Mander, his hands closing around Mander's throat. Mander refused to fight back, his hands remaining at his side. As Mander's knees buckled and he sank to the ground, Scott's face broke into an evil grin that only lasted as long as it took the laser bolt to blast his head into mush.

All eyes fell on Private First Class Kalen Richardson who stood, his sidearm in his hand still pointing to where Scott had been standing.

"I'm—I'm sorry," he said, "I didn't have time to put it in the stun setting."

Mander smiled and croaked through his damaged throat, "The Lord's justice has been served, my young friend! Do not be sorry, for you have discovered your purpose! You were preserved from the crash to be the Lord's tool of deliverance! Let us rejoice in the sovereign hand of our Lord!"

A high-pitched cheer went up from the Qatixi people as Kalen pushed his sidearm back into its holster. He looked down at Captain Peabody who flashed a rare grin at him.

"Nice shooting, Private. I guess we can skip the discipline for losing that sidearm before?"

As adrenaline faded from his body, Kalen had no response but a weary smile.

*Under a dying star, in a one-person shelter, with a robot for company, Ozero can run from his past. But when a visitor appears, he discovers he can either seek revenge or forgiveness . . . the choice is his.*

# HAVEN
## LAUREN SMYTH

# CHAPTER ONE
# KICKSTART

*pent most of the day categorizing specimens. Haven't seen anything alive except for the bamboo—not the kind of bamboo we have at home, of course. More on that in my lab notes. I hope they pick me up soon.*

—Day #330

Ozero closed his journal with a sigh. What was the point in writing when he had nothing left to say? He couldn't even remember how many days he'd been trapped on his lonely little planet. Three hundred was a maddening understatement.

His desk was lined with specimens he should've been classifying, but he couldn't focus on his work. Each time he picked up a leaf to analyze it, he noticed all its imperfections. There was a crack where the membrane should have been smooth, or a vein that was just the wrong shade of purple. No matter how hard he searched, he couldn't find one that he considered "perfect."

"If I go back to Earth," he mused aloud, staring at the tiny cracks in the plastic table, "people are going to think I'm crazy." *As if they don't already.*

He stood up, savoring the sound of his boots clicking on the floor—that was the only manmade sound, except his own voice, he'd heard in a while—and paced around the pod.

"*When* I go back to Earth," he corrected hastily. "They'll come for me soon."

He had the unsettling feeling that they wouldn't, but that was irrational, and he knew it. His contract was only valid for a year. Once that time was up, his employer would have to retrieve him or face legal repercussions. The Clerical Court might even get involved if the process dragged on too long.

His contract was taped to the wall above his bed. Every morning, he got up and checked to see if it were still there, and he'd read it over again.

KICKSTART BIOLOGY, INC.

*Such a stupid name for a multi-billion*—dollar? Euro? Credit? Something else? The fact that he couldn't remember his own currency was just another proof he was going insane.

> *1. The undersigned promises to remain in the employment of Kickstart Biology, Inc., until a year has passed or until he chooses to terminate the contract—whichever is later.*

There were twenty more obscure points he'd unconditionally agreed to, but the first was the only one that mattered. He tore his eyes away from the contract, trying not to question himself about why he ever agreed to come here. *Don't do what you always do.*

The 'sun'—if it counted as a sun, because the light it produced was red and not very sun-like at all—was already setting. Ozero's hand accidentally brushed the ice-cold window, and he shivered. He paused to appreciate the beauty of the sunset—*starset?*—but there was none. At least, none that he could see. It looked the same as it did every night. There wasn't much of an atmosphere to scatter the light and make a proper 'starset.' It just reflected obliquely off the ground where it was clear, and off the waxy purple plant leaves where it wasn't.

Suddenly lonely, he decided he wanted to have a real conversation, even if it couldn't be with another human. And he was due for his daily evaluation anyway—though he preferred not to think about that.

He went back inside, wrapped himself in a blanket, and pressed a button on the wall beside him.

A flickering blue screen appeared in the air in front of him, and he adjusted it until it was at his eye level. It hung immobile for a few seconds, and then a face appeared on the screen—a young woman's face, framed with artificially smooth brown hair. At least her expressions changed like a real person's, even if the computer couldn't quite smooth out the robotic movements that betrayed her mechanical origins.

"How are you doing?" she asked, with a friendly wave.

"What's your name?" asked Ozero.

"Thank you for asking! You can call me whatever you w—"

"What's your *name*?" he insisted. It wasn't a name if he got to choose it himself.

The avatar paused, almost like she understood his frustration. "You can call me Mia."

"Mia," he repeated obediently.

"Do you mind if I run a quick psychological evaluation?" Her tone was gentle and persuasive. "It won't take long, and you can keep talking while I work."

"Sure," said Ozero gloomily. The chatbots never wasted time on small talk. Three hundred days ago, when he was back in civilization, he would've thanked them for it, but now it made him feel even more lonely.

"Please accept the prompt on your watch so I can access your vital signs," said the avatar.

Ozero did as he was instructed and leaned back against his pillows, searching for something to say.

"So, Mia, do you know what these plants are?" He pointed to his desk. "If you just told me, it would save me a lot of time."

"I'm sorry, I don't know. But you'd be bored if you had nothing to do, wouldn't you?"

*Spoken like a true therapist,* Ozero thought ruefully.

"Why do you say that?" he asked.

"Everyone gets bored. That's why work exists. All play and no work is—"

Yet another cliché. Mia paused, sensing his annoyance.

"Your evaluation is done," she said, raising one eyebrow stiffly. "Let's talk about the results."

"Right." Ozero sighed.

"You're stressed," said Mia. Her eyes locked on Ozero's, and he glanced away uncomfortably. *What a surprise.* "Do you need to increase the dosage of your medicines?"

"No," he insisted. "We've been over this."

Mia smiled. "But there are no side effects. You'd feel better if you took them."

"No. I won't."

There was a long pause, and Ozero cursed himself for feeling guilty over being rude to a robot.

"Listen, Mia," he said roughly, trying not to sound panicked, "you know I wish I felt better. I really do. But I'll never be able to join the clerics if I keep taking those drugs. By the time Kickstart comes to pick me up, I need to have stopped taking them altogether."

"What do the clerics have to do with this?"

Ozero knew that she knew the story as well as he did. All his personal information had already been stored in the computer, and anything it didn't know had been dragged out of him over the weeks he'd been on his planet.

But, reluctantly, staring into Mia's mesmerizing, flickering eyes, he spoke.

"Of course, the clerics don't want me. Why would they? I see the imperfections in everything. Those bamboo leaves. The walls. The floors, even though they look like they're perfectly square and white—they don't satisfy me. Nothing does."

"So you clean the floors, don't you?" prompted Mia. She'd heard all this before.

"I scrub them for hours at a time." Ozero wondered if that was really such a problem, or if he was just trying to sound dramatic and ill enough to justify himself. *After all, being tidy is a good thing, isn't it?* He rushed to keep talking before his mind could get sidetracked. "I classify leaves, and I keep gathering samples of the same things over and over. I can't stop."

"But that doesn't mean something's wrong with you," Mia cooed. "It's merely a symptom of OCD. Why aren't you willing to take the medications?"

"O-C-D." Ozero spelled the acronym out, as if that would help him understand it better. "It's in the name. Obsessive. Compulsive. Disorder. Of course, it means something's wrong with me. If people see me and think I'm crazy, something's wrong with me." He pinched his lips shut. "I need to overcome it on my own, without the medicine."

This time Mia's smile was pitying, annoying Ozero even more. "That's not how it works."

He'd finally had enough. His hands reached for the flickering blue screen almost before he noticed, but they closed on air. There was a buzz, and the screen faded away, taking Mia with it. Her voice glitched and went silent.

His eyes drifted to the specimens on the desk. Guilty, guilty for not working—that was how he felt all the time, even when he knew that he'd earned a break. It was already dark outside, and he was supposed to be asleep. But he got up and went to the desk anyway. He needed something to occupy his hands while his thoughts were elsewhere.

It's a pity. Are you sure you wouldn't get distracted when things get tough? What do you think would happen if you fixated on something and couldn't pay attention when people needed your help? The choice is yours. Do you think you could handle it? If you can answer 'yes' honestly, we'll take you. But remember, you're responsible for your own actions.

Ozero didn't know when he'd turned that into "it's your fault if anything goes wrong." But even if he hadn't, how could he have answered the cleric recruiter's question? He might as well have asked

Ozero if he'd detonate a bomb. He didn't know what would happen, and he didn't want to.

For weeks he'd worried about it, wondering if he was making the right decision. And eventually, he fixated on an excuse. *You can't join the clerics because you might be a liability.* But that would've meant the end of the story, and his mind never gave him that much of a break. So he added a loophole: *It's the medicines that make you drowsy. If you could stop taking those, you wouldn't have to worry. You could join the clerics with a clear conscience.*

Ozero had promptly stopped taking the medications. That was the blessing and curse of his illness—when he fixated on something, there was no taking his mind off it. When his mother brought the medicines, he made her take them back to the kitchen. She'd yelled at him, but that was a sacrifice he was prepared to make.

He woke up during the night in a cold sweat. *The locks on the doors.* He hadn't checked them before he went to sleep. What if he hadn't been careful and the doors weren't closed all the way? What if someone got in and hurt his mother and sister? What if —? What if —?

He got up and checked the locks, careful not to brush them with his hand as he stepped away. Who knew what would happen if he did? When he turned to go back upstairs to his bedroom, his sister was sitting on the step like a tiny wraith in the moonlight. Her shoulders were shaking, and his cheeks reddened as he realized she was laughing at him.

So he went back to the kitchen and took his medicines, swallowing them in a single, self-pitying gulp that made his eyes water. He wiped away his tears and trudged upstairs, determined not to get out of bed again no matter what dire consequence he might face if he didn't.

*And if you hadn't done that, would things have been any different?* The voice in Ozero's head startled him so much that he almost dropped the specimen he was holding.

*If you'd stopped the medicines, would you have checked the locks again the next night?*

## CHAPTER TWO

# THE VISITOR ON A LONELY PLANET

Ozero woke up the next morning with a weight of guilt on his chest that he couldn't quite place at first. Then he remembered.

He reached over to his nightstand and downed a pill, not bothering to drink any water with it. Maybe if he didn't drink, the medicine wouldn't absorb as well, and he'd really be taking less of it.

A few minutes later, he felt calm enough to step out of bed and peek out the window. He knew what he was about to see. Same blinding, bright red light. Same "bamboos" with their waxy leaves dead still.

That's what he expected, but that's not what he saw.

Instead of the plants, a face was staring in his window—a face partly covered by a shaded visor that only showed the wearer's icy cyan eyes. They stared blankly at him, and for a split second Ozero wondered if he was somehow hallucinating a mechanized version of his own reflection.

Then he screamed and stumbled back against the wall.

"If I'm hallucinating . . . " he panted, putting his hands on the chilly floor just to remind himself that the world around him was real. One deep breath, and then another. He had to think clearly.

He'd noticed all the details of the face, right down to the subtle reflection of his own terrified expression in the staring eyes. He even remembered thinking, in the flash before he panicked, that he'd read about eyes like those in a book somewhere. Maybe he wasn't crazy after all. But if not, then how . . . ?

There was a knock on the door, and Ozero started like it was a gunshot.

Slowly, he stood up and opened the door. There he saw a person—a real person, however unlikely. And Ozero immediately noticed that they were missing the all-important radiation protection shield that blocked the light of the dying star the planet orbited.

"Please let me in," said a tinny voice. It seemed to come from a speaker somewhere in the visor. "Please . . . " The voice trailed away, and Ozero barely had time to jump aside as the figure crashed across his doorstep and lay still on the ground.

He peeked cautiously around the doorframe. Nobody else was nearby, but he could see footprints headed toward him from the forest of bamboo in front of his shelter. If this person, whoever they were, had come in a spaceship, it must have landed far enough away that he hadn't heard or seen it. He wondered when they'd landed, and how far they'd had to walk, and how they'd known he was here.

Then, getting a grip on his nerves, he dragged the body inside and shut the door behind him. The visor covering the face fogged slightly, and Ozero sighed with relief. At least they were still alive.

The first order of business was stripping off the irradiated outerwear—a long military trench coat that had been designed for the close quarters of a spaceship, not the harsh elements of this planet's surface. It had little pinpoint holes burned into the fabric, which looked like they might've come from a hot, mildly radioactive sandstorm that had struck two days before. Ozero winced. So they'd been outside for a while.

He pulled the jacket off and put it in the incinerator. It was a shame to waste, but he couldn't risk being exposed to the radiation that it might've picked up. Then, gently, he detached the visor from the face.

It was more wrinkled and scarred than Ozero's. Still, the man couldn't have been much older. Even if Ozero couldn't have guessed that from his features, he might've known from the eyes. Bright and blue and wide open, they stared at the ceiling, and there was a faint imprint of a brand name on the retinas. "Kickstart."

These implants were a new technology that hadn't been around long, and they were made to strengthen the user's vision to pinpoint accuracy at long distances. Ozero had once read that people with the implants couldn't read, but they could hit a target five hundred yards away using a sniper rifle without a scope. A useful skill for the right kind of person.

Ozero put the visor into a biohazard bag, then knelt on the floor and slapped the man's cheek. "You need to wake up."

No response.

He put his hand on the man's chest and turned on his watch. Heart rate, normal—well, normal given the circumstances. Breathing, a little fast and shallow, but nothing serious. No bleeding. Yet something was clearly wrong.

"Warning." His watch screen flashed rapidly. "Radiation approaching dangerous levels. Leave the area immediately."

Ozero felt as if he could sense the radioactive particles hitting his skin. Reluctantly, he left the man on the floor and donned the heavy suit he wore when he went outside. It reeked of biohazard soap, which he used to clean the suit whenever he brought it back in doors. The smell reminded him that now he'd have to clean his entire shelter with that bitter-smelling soap, and then he wouldn't be able to sleep because of the fumes, and he'd wake up in the middle of the night thinking about that tiny patch on the floor he'd missed. He'd do a radiation-area calculation to figure out his exposure level, and by the time he finished that, he might as well have cleaned the whole room again, because he'd be trembling with fear and unable to go back to sleep anyway.

His internal monologue didn't last more than a few seconds, though it felt like a year's worth of anxiety. Just as he finished strapping on the helmet, he heard a noise behind him. He turned to see the man propped with his back against the wall, pointing his gun at Ozero.

"Whoa." Ozero raised his hands disarmingly, trying to stifle the nervousness in his throat. "I'm the only one here. There's nothing to be afraid of." *For you, anyway.* "Let's talk."

The man didn't say a word.

Ozero gulped. "What's your name?"

There was a long pause, and then he answered. "Kem."

"Nice to meet you, Kem. I'm Ozero," he said with nervous cheerfulness. "Can you please put that gun away?"

This time the pause was even longer, but just when Ozero was convinced he was about to feel a bullet in his chest, Kem clicked on the safety and placed the gun on the floor in front of him.

"Don't pick that up," he said, resting his head against the wall. "I don't trust you, but I don't have a choice."

Ozero edged toward the door just in case he needed to make a run for it. "You really should change clothes. My biometric scans indicate that you're irradiated. It's the star, you know. It's dying and it gives off a lot of radiation. And the sandstorm the other day . . . that didn't help." He wondered if his chatter sounded as terrified as he felt.

"Got anything I can borrow?"

"You'll need to shower first," he said cautiously. "Do you think you can . . . ?"

"Did you scan me?"

"You mean a biometric scan? I tried, but it didn't finish. I had to put on a radiation suit just to get near you." His confidence was returning slowly as Kem made no move to retrieve his weapon. "I'll run the scan again."

Kem's cyan eyes lit up and he stared at Ozero, who froze obediently in place. "No need. I know what's wrong with me. Radiation poisoning and a head that nearly got split open on a rock. Some iodine pills and painkillers should fix me up."

Ozero couldn't shake the feeling that he could physically sense the radiation striking his skin, and he was eager to get rid of his dangerous guest. So, keeping his eyes on the gun, he backed toward the wall and slid open the bathroom door. "I'll put some clothes and a towel out for you. Use the soap in the green bottle. That'll get rid of the radiation."

The man tried to stand up, but failed pathetically, and Ozero didn't dare get close enough to help. So Kem wobbled across the floor on his hands and knees, pausing occasionally to push his stringy, unwashed hair out of his eyes. With a final scowl and warning not to touch his weapon, he slammed the bathroom door behind him and disappeared.

Ozero sighed and looked down at his trembling hands. Trembling because of the radiation, probably. That was ridiculous and he knew it—he hadn't been exposed long enough to have any physical symptoms—but he couldn't convince himself that he was safe. So he found a sponge and his special soap and started scrubbing.

He was still working when Kem emerged from the bathroom, the expression on his face as sullen as before. Now he was dressed in Ozero's clothes, which were comically small and made him look squeezed. He picked up his gun and shoved it in his pocket—or at least, tried to before he realized that the pockets were stretched too tight—and then held out a hand.

"Iodine," he demanded curtly.

Ozero went to the first aid kit and handed him a brown glass bottle. "One every twenty-four hours."

Kem downed a pill and put the bottle in his pocket. Then he sat down on the bed and placed his weapon on the floor beside his feet. Apparently, he wasn't planning to let it out of his sight again.

"Thanks for your help." The words came out like they were forced.

"Don't thank me. But what happened to you?" Ozero continued scrubbing, not looking at his guest. He knew he'd snap something rude about sitting on the bed if he did—he couldn't stand it when other people touched his comforter.

"Spaceship malfunction. Landed here two days ago."

"You were the only one who survived?"

Kem eyed him suspiciously. "Yes. There was a carbon dioxide leak."

"The ventilation system failed?"

"That's right."

"And so you crash landed?" Ozero asked.

"What? No. The ship's in one piece. I was going to try to fix it before I started getting sick." Kem wrapped Ozero's blanket around his shoulders and huddled against the wall. "You a crash investigator or what? Gonna write me up?"

Ozero wanted to laugh, but the sound choked in his throat.

"You should get some rest," he told Kem, hiding his confusion behind a cough. "You can take my bed for tonight. Is there anything else you need?"

"Food."

Without a word, Ozero put a bouillon cube into a cup and mixed it with hot water from the tap. Anything else would make him sick. He stuck a metal spoon into the brew and handed it to Kem.

"I'll leave you alone," he said, observing that his guest was about to protest the frugal meal. With a friendly wave he drew the curtains around his bed, locking them shut with his watch. He didn't want Kem to get up in the middle of the night, shoot him, and leave with his ship and supplies.

Then he went outside.

He'd never been so excited to see the plants. They were tall and shiny and proud, and they were a non-distracting place for him to think about what he was going to do next.

Something about Kem's story didn't sit right. For starters, there was no way a spaceship would have a carbon dioxide leak. Carbon monoxide, maybe. The mistake could've been a slip of the tongue, but even if it was, Ozero thought the whole story was highly unlikely—there wasn't a single recorded case of ventilation system failure in the last ten years. What were the odds that Kem was the first, and that he'd just happened to make a safe landing on Ozero's planet? And how had he survived if everyone else on his ship suffocated? Ozero was determined to investigate.

He started by following the footprints. Kem's shoes hadn't sunk deeply into the sand because of the low gravity, but there hadn't been any wind, and there were very few other active environmental decay processes. So, even though the prints were almost flat, Ozero could just barely follow them.

But they wound around endlessly, and Ozero was soon completely lost. Clearly, Kem hadn't known where he was or where he was going. It was fun being that ancient character Daniel Boone the Expert Tracker for a while, but Ozero was in a hurry, and he needed to get back to his shelter before Kem woke up and found that he was locked in. He didn't seem like the type to be above shooting the lock and, possibly, his host. The thought made Ozero shiver.

He pulled out his watch and scanned the planet's surface for anomalous objects.

It only took a few seconds for the computer to register Kem's ship—a solid metal object only about a hundred yards away. So Kem had wandered in the bushes for two days, while Ozero's shelter was less than a mile from his landing spot. If he'd had a scanner like Ozero's, he shouldn't have gotten lost. All properly equipped spaceships had them, and properly equipped meant Federation approved.

Ozero picked up his pace. A few minutes later, he came to a clearing in the bamboo—a clearing that hadn't existed until Kem's spaceship had landed and flattened everything around it. The spaceship itself was made of old, rusted black metal that didn't look like it should have been flying it all.

Ozero inspected the logo on the side. In roughly painted letters, it read:

EXCISION

"Excision . . . cutting something out?" Ozero mused. "This isn't the original logo."

He tried the door, and to his surprise, it swung open. He didn't understand why Kem wouldn't have locked it when he left, but when he looked closer, he saw that the door didn't have a lock at all. Another breach of Federation protocol. Spaceships without locks often came apart when entering unfamiliar atmospheres—their doors simply weren't strong enough to stand the increasing pressure, unless they were reenforced with standard alloy locks.

The ship was much smaller inside than Ozero expected. There was nothing but a cot in the back, screwed tightly to the floor, and a pilot's seat in front. Only one seat. Why would Kem have lied about having a crew when there was obviously never anyone else onboard?

Increasingly uneasy, Ozero crawled inside and examined his surroundings. Sterile cleanliness. Burn marks on the walls, suggesting they'd overheated. This spaceship should've been retired long ago.

There was a photograph taped to the wall beside the cot. Ozero scrutinized it closely. It showed a happy little family of three—a mother, a daughter, and a son—posing with wide-eyed smiles outside a house.

*That house.*

Ozero's mouth went dry. That house . . . the number beside the door . . .

Suddenly the faces of the mother and daughter blurred. The only one he could still see through the tears collecting in his eyes was the son's.

His own face.

He tore the photo down from the wall and crushed it in his gloved hand. Now it didn't matter why Kem had lied. All Ozero needed were answers, immediate answers for why the family he had lost was memorialized in this man's forsaken spaceship.

# CHAPTER THREE
# HAUNTED MEMORIES

*If you'd stopped the medicines, would you have checked the locks again the next night?*

If he had, he wouldn't have woken up to the sound of crying. A soft, gentle, almost comforting crying coming from his mother's room. Ozero had listened for a few moments, spellbound, wondering if he was imagining the sound. He'd never heard his mother cry before. Maybe his sister was crying and had run to her for comfort— but if so, why couldn't he hear his mother's voice comforting her? And his sister never cried, either. She was a big girl—bigger and braver than he was, he'd always thought, because she didn't need medicine to act like a "normal" person.

He got up and tiptoed to her room, following the sound until he peeked through the crack in her door. She was sitting on the floor, her back against the bedframe, her knees hugged to her chest, rocking back and forth. His sister was nowhere in sight.

"I don't know what to tell the kids," his mother sobbed softly, holding her watch close to her mouth. Ozero wondered who she was talking to. "There's nothing left. Not a single thing. I tried to catch him, but he was so fast, and the police wouldn't have gotten here in time.

I've no choice but to wait until the morning—but in the meantime, what can I do?" Her plea for help sounded so desperate that little Ozero, though he had no idea what was wrong, felt tears coming to his eyes. He slid down against the doorframe and sobbed silently, half hoping his mother would hear him and come to give him a hug.

Maybe he'd been born with OCD just for that specific moment, so he would've double-checked the lock on the back door. That, the police told him later, was how the burglar got inside the house. And when he came downstairs the next morning, he saw that there was nothing left but emptiness. A sofa, which had been too heavy for the burglar to carry, and a half empty bottle of milk in the fridge. Their soundproof bedroom walls, specifically installed to help them sleep peacefully at night despite the noise of the city outside, had prevented them from waking up until hours after the burglar was already gone. Ozero's mother had gone downstairs to see that the little they had was theirs no longer.

Ozero's birthday was the next day. He celebrated with a tiny cup of milk that his sister complained tasted bitter. That was all they had left, and there was no way for them to get anything more.

"You're the man of the house now." That was what Ozero's father, an eternal wanderer and dreamer of what he couldn't achieve, had told him the last time he left on an interstellar voyage. That had been two years before the robbery, and they hadn't heard a word from him since. Ozero's mother couldn't work because she'd injured her back years ago and had never paid for surgery, and his sister was too young. Ozero was almost too young, but there was one place that would take him. Kickstart. That was the reason he'd signed his life away to come here. That was how, in the space of about seven years, he'd gone from "little Ozero" who cried in sympathy with his mother to the lonely, dissatisfied man he was now.

His mother had begged him not to leave. Said they'd work something out, said he needed to go to school, said he shouldn't have to worry about money at such a young age. It was all platitudes, meant to keep him at home where he'd never be able to achieve anything beyond his poverty and frustration. In retrospect, had he left because he wanted to make money for his family, or because he wanted a chance to be better than them? He didn't know, and probably never would. What mattered was that he left.

His sister, ever the fiery one, flew into a rage and vowed never to speak to him again "if you leave us sitting here in this rotting dump." No matter how many times Ozero explained he was leaving for her, not for himself, neither he nor his sister believed it.

The more they disagreed, the more they tore their relationship apart. Eventually Ozero's mother had enough of the fighting. If he was so bent on leaving, she said, he could leave, as long as he made a solemn promise to come back. He deserved his freedom, he had to go out and live his life, she'd raised him well— all the things mothers say to convince themselves their child isn't leaving for good.

Ozero pretended to make the promise. But he didn't mean to go back. Or maybe, he reasoned to convince himself he wasn't lying, he'd go back once he achieved what he wanted. He couldn't help thinking that made him just like his wandering father, who had left his family to fend for themselves while he went off on adventures around the galaxy. A reverse knight in shining armor, Ozero thought bitterly.

Things would never have ended up like this if Ozero hadn't run away. He wouldn't have run away if it hadn't been for that lonely, stale cup of milk on his birthday. And he would've had cake for his birthday if their house hadn't been robbed. And his house wouldn't have been robbed if it wasn't for the *robber*.

# CHAPTER FOUR
## THE CHOICE PRESENTED

"You owe me an explanation." He was surprised how calm his voice sounded. It was more like the robot's voice than his own—stiff and preprogrammed. Ozero had been rehearsing what he was going to say the whole way back to his shelter.

He unlocked his curtains and opened them to reveal a sleepy Kem, rubbing his cyan eyes and rumbling wrathfully.

"You've got some nerve locking me in," he snapped. "Federation citizens are supposed to trust each other."

"You expect me to trust you after you lied?" Ozero grabbed Kem's weapon up off the nightstand and held it pointed at the ceiling. He had no idea how to use it, but he had a feeling adrenaline was the only weapon he'd need if worst came to worst. His fingers felt a switch on the side—a safety, perhaps?—and he pressed it, half expecting it to fire. Nothing happened.

"Care to explain why you're illegally operating a spaceship in Federation space?" he continued, trying not to raise his voice. It wasn't time for that yet. "Why you lied about having an entire crew die of ventilation failure? And most importantly"—Ozero shoved the crumpled photo in Kem's face—"why this was on your wall?"

Silence.

"Who are those people?" asked Kem at last. "I can't see them."

Ozero held the photo further from his eyes.

"Your family?"

"How do you know that?"

Kem's gaze flicked bath and forth between the photo and Ozero. "Because you're the boy in that picture. You still look like a child."

"Tell me why you have this." Ozero pointed the gun at Kem's forehead, his finger trembling over the trigger guard.

There was a long pause, until Kem finally smiled. "Your mind is already made up. It wouldn't make a difference even if I told you I'm an old family friend, would it? You think I did something terrible. It's written all over your face."

"I haven't decided yet," said Ozero. His fingers tightened.

"Why would I have a picture of your family if I'm *not* your family?" said Kem. His eyes flitted around the room like he was trying to think of what to say next. Ozero traced their path—first to the door, then to the window, and finally briefly at the gun. Then he looked straight at Ozero. "Fine. I'll tell you the truth, if it's the last thing you want to know. But I'll have to kill you once I tell you."

Ozero scoffed, nearly choking on the paralyzing fear in his chest. "You won't get far without a radiation suit."

"I'll borrow yours." Kem stood up slowly, with his hands above his head. "I'm not your long-lost uncle. I'm the one who robbed your family. What's the point in lying? You'd guess the truth anyway—it's not like there's any other reason for me to have that picture. And my spaceship was an execution ship. I wasn't meant to survive a landing."

Momentarily stunned, Ozero felt his grip on the weapon weaken. *The Federation does things like that . . . ? The Federation executes people . . . like this?*

But Kem didn't wait around to him to figure out the answer. With one quick leap, he was up off the bed, his hand slicing upward like a knife and knocking the gun out of Ozero's uncertain hands.

"You know nothing about me." He pushed his knee hard into Ozero's chest, knocking him against the wall and stunning him. Then he wrapped his hands around his throat, not quite firmly enough to choke him, but enough to scare him into freezing. "You don't know what made me do it. You can't pass judgement on me." Kem's voice seethed with frustration. "And you're lucky none of you woke up that day. If you had, I would've killed you all. I was just that desperate."

Ozero tried to peel the fingers off his throat. With increasing desperation, he realized he might as well have been trying to pull off a noose. "If you kill me . . . I'll know exactly what kind of person you are," he choked. "And then your excuses won't matter."

He wasn't ready to die. Another wave of terror washed over him, paralyzing his muscles and forcing him to relax. His eyes met Kem's. For a split second he thought the killer might relent when he saw the fear in his eyes—might take pity on someone who couldn't hurt him anyway. But as soon as he saw the flash of cyan, Ozero realized that Kem couldn't see him. They were too close together.

And then it happened.

Kem reached behind him to pick up the gun Ozero had dropped. There was a deafening explosion, and Kem screamed—a hoarse scream of pain and surprise. Just as suddenly, he went silent and collapsed onto Ozero's shoulder. His hands fell to his side, releasing Ozero's throat.

Ozero felt himself smothering under the man's weight. Struggling for air, he pushed him aside. Something seemed to snap in his side as he did so, and he gasped. Every breath ached.

Propping himself against the wall, he examined his injuries. There was blood on his coat—Kem's? or was it his? His head was starting to spin. He couldn't let himself pass out. If he did, Kem might wake up first and kill him in his sleep. He had to stay awake . . . had to kill Kem before he woke up . . .

He stretched out his hand to pick up the weapon Kem had dropped, but before his fingers touched it his head became so heavy that he dropped it to his chest. His ears rang, and he toppled to the floor.

# CHAPTER FIVE
## THE DECISION MADE

Ozero woke to searing pain in his side. He pressed his hand against it, vaguely wondering if that would stop his organs from falling out. It came away soaked with blood. So Kem's wild shot had somehow hit them both.

He glanced over at Kem, who was still stretched unmoving across the floor. When he saw the gun, he guessed immediately what had happened. Kem hadn't seen him press the safety switch while he'd been holding it, and since he couldn't see up close anyway, he had accidentally brushed the trigger, careless because he assumed the weapon wasn't armed. What a stupid mistake. He should have known better.

Ozero crawled toward him, wincing every time his knees brushed the floor. He slid his hand onto Kem's neck and waited. Nothing at first, and then . . . the firm pulse under his fingers startled him.

*Put on your oxygen mask before assisting other passengers*—that's what they always said on the publicly accessible travel spaceships, in case there was ever a leak in the oxygen system. It hadn't happened to Ozero, but he remembered the warning. So he left Kem and dragged himself into the bathroom, where he kept a cabinet full of antiseptics and bandages. He patched himself up, rubbing a generous helping of numbing lotion into his wound. Upon closer inspection, it wasn't very deep—nothing more than a jagged scratch.

He'd passed out from the shock, not from blood loss. The pain faded away as the cream took effect, and he wrapped himself in a white cotton bandage. Then he propped his hands against the sink, pulled himself to his feet, and collected a handful of bandages and antiseptics for Kem.

When he went back into the main room and saw Kem sleeping peacefully on the floor, a slow—very slow—trickle of blood seeping from under his chest, he paused.

Why should he help?

He *shouldn't* help. His family was destroyed because of this man, assuming he'd told the truth and why would he lie about something like that? Even if he had, he'd tried to kill Ozero, too. There was enough evidence captured on the cameras in Ozero's shelter to get him imprisoned for life. So why should Ozero let him go?

*You wanted to be a cleric. But you're not. You don't get to make decisions like this.*

Ozero bit his lip indecisively.

*Isn't this just me taking responsibility for my actions, like they said I should?*

*This isn't what they meant, and you know it. You don't get to decide who lives or dies.*

*If you kill him, you're just like him.*

Reluctantly, Ozero opened the bottle of antiseptic.

*Who do you want to be proud of you?*

He'd never asked himself that question before. He paused to consider. If Kem bled out on the floor while he was thinking, it wouldn't be his fault, would it?

It was just another excuse. He took a step toward Kem in a momentary feeling of guilt.

*Your mother and sister, or the clerics?*

*Or both?*

*You can show the clerics you respect them if you make the right decision.*
*It may not be too late for you.*

It was too late. Ozero didn't have any doubts about that. But did he still have something to prove? To whom? To himself? To the clerics? To his family, who had probably already given up on his return?

He wanted to be like the clerics. Strong, just, people that everyone looked up to because they were *needed*. Ozero had never been needed. Even now, he was stranded on a lonely planet because there hadn't been anywhere better to send him. He was expendable, and everyone in his life had let him know it. Even Kickstart Biology, as little as their opinion mattered.

And now Kem needed him.

Cursing under his breath, he darted forward and examined Kem's wound. His had gone deeper than Ozero's—right through his ribcage and exiting through his chest. His pulse was fast and erratic, and Ozero wondered if he was going to wake up at all.

He couldn't call for help. It was just the two of them, and Ozero got to decide if he lived or died. He could practically hear the cleric's voice in his head now: *If you want to be like us, do you trust us?* And he hated it, but he listened.

He glanced at the picture he'd dropped on the floor when Kem attacked him. A happy little family, they had been, and would never be again. And now here he was, patching up the man who'd taken it all away. Kem had said something about Ozero failing to understand why he'd done it. Well, did it really matter? Nothing could absolve him.

Still, Ozero was sure of three things: he didn't want to go to jail for murder, he didn't want to lose faith in the clerics, and he didn't want to live with any more on his conscience than he already had. He pushed the picture under the bed with his foot, laid out the bandages on the floor in front of him, and got to work.

At least now he could say he tried.

# CHAPTER SIX
# THE CLERIC

It was two months before anyone arrived to take him home—ten days after his contract expired, to be exact. Ozero counted down the days with growing certainty that nobody would ever come. Then, one day, he heard rustling in the bamboo. It was a rescue ship, with the colorful logo KICKSTART BIOLOGY painted across the side.

Ozero was so happy he cried. And then, when he was finished crying, he tore his contract off the wall and ripped it to shreds. Perhaps it wasn't the wisest way of celebrating, but he was so relieved that he didn't have to wake up and look at it first thing every morning that he couldn't help himself.

From his cot next to the window, Kem saw the ship coming, too. And he saw Ozero sob, at which he rolled his cyan eyes and hid his face against the wall. He didn't say anything. In fact, he hadn't said a word since the day he'd woken up a few hours after Ozero finished patching him up. It was clear he was ashamed of himself, though Ozero couldn't tell if it was because he was embarrassed at accidentally shooting himself or because he wished he hadn't been saved at all.

There was a cleric guard aboard the ship. Ozero met him privately while everyone else was packing up and explained who Kem was,

117

how he'd found him, and what evidence he'd captured on his security cameras. The cleric's eyes widened.

"So, he landed here to save himself," he mused. "And just happened to run into you. That's ironic justice."

Ozero nodded silently, wondering if the cleric was about to ask why Kem was expected to be his problem now. He didn't seem like the kind of person to waste words, though. Ozero realized he was letting his intrusive thoughts get the better of him again and snapped to attention just in time to catch the cleric's question.

"But you still didn't let him die. Why not?"

Ozero licked his lips uncertainly. Whatever he was about to say, he was sure it was going to sound stupid. The cleric waited patiently, and finally Ozero said, "I always wanted to be one of you. I thought that if I couldn't let you do your job—pass justice and all that—then I wasn't showing much respect." He paused. "And of course, I also didn't want to go to jail for manslaughter."

The cleric laughed. For a split second, his deep, ocean-blue eyes reflected in the white, fluorescent light as cyan, and Ozero flinched.

"Why didn't you join us?" he asked. "You would've made a great initiate. You acted thoughtfully in a dangerous situation, which is all we could possibly ask for."

This time Ozero hesitated even longer. "I have OCD," he said at last. "One of the cleric recruiters told me that if I ever made a bad decision because of that, I'd have to live with the consequences. I didn't think I could." He studied the cleric's eyes. *They're just blue. Dark blue, like . . . like your neighbor's front door. Not cyan. He doesn't even look like Kem.*

"There's no cure for that," said the cleric gently. "But don't you think you've shown that you can overcome it? All you had to do was realize that you don't have to do everything by yourself. You trusted the clerics enough to save this man's life, and you believed we'd help you if you waited for us to come. You probably thought you had to save yourself, but you didn't. We're all here to help you and see that you get the justice you deserve. You knew that, and you were able to make the right decision on your own." A smile crossed his face. "To stay out of jail. Regardless of your motive, you did the right thing."

"True . . ." Ozero didn't know how to respond. He kept his eyes fixed on the floor.

"So do you want to try again?"

"What?"

"Do you want to go back to training?"

Ozero shook his head and shrugged. "I'm twenty-three. Don't you think I'm a little old?"

"Absolutely not," said the cleric firmly. "Nobody is too old for a second chance at life. Tell you what, why don't you train with me?"

Ozero raised his eyes. "With you? You mean . . . I can shadow you?"

The cleric nodded. "Eventually, you'll be able to work on your own. And besides, it's custom for a First Class to take on an initiate. I haven't found anyone yet, so I'd be honored if you'd agree."

"You really think I can do it?"

"I wouldn't ask you to come if I didn't."

Ozero could feel his face turning red with excitement. "Well . . . my contract is expired. There's nowhere else I need to be. Take me with you."

"You seem decisive, at least," chuckled the cleric. "That's a good sign. I'll take you back to Earth and have you sign the paperwork. Then we'll head to Protocol Alpha for training. Just be patient until then, and I promise you'll get to do everything you've wanted and more."

"Wait." Ozero stopped him. "What's your name?"

The cleric offered his hand to shake. "Malachi."

# CHAPTER SEVEN
# THE GOD WHO SAVES

Six months later, Ozero watched Kem's trial. He sat in the very back bench, all the way in the corner, where he could jump out the window if he felt he couldn't stand it anymore.

Nothing could ever force Ozero to pity the man. Not respect for the clerics, or himself, or his family. Ozero didn't believe he'd ever understand, or forget, no matter how hard he tried to remember that the only one hurt by his stubbornness was himself. And if he ever *did* pity Kem, it would have to be a choice, not a feeling that arose spontaneously out of nowhere.

But Kem was, maybe, less of a demon than Ozero had believed. He was only seventeen when he broke into Ozero's house, intending to rob the kitchen—not for money, he insisted, but for food only. When he realized that Ozero's family had no more food than he did, besides a badly decorated, cheap birthday cake, he'd made off with everything valuable he could find.

"After all," he said sullenly when cross-questioned, "I had to eat. And I didn't want to rely on charity, because there were plenty of people who deserved it more than I did." Ozero rather charitably interpreted this to mean that there were plenty of people who wouldn't steal, no matter what, and they deserved another option.

Just before he left the house, Kem took their photo off the refrigerator as a guilty souvenir. An eternal reminder of his sin, which he was already regretting as he stared at the happy little family and wished he could be more like them. He wanted to forget, but he was too guilty to let go.

He ran from the Federation and stayed on the run until he reached a planet several light years from Earth. It happened to be a planet where there were no clerics, a planet where people who had something to hide from fit right in. Kem had no choice but to become their unwilling ally. His theft wouldn't mean anything if he starved after all.

They gave him his new pair of eyes and forced him to start stealing again, pirating unwitting ships that came too close to the planet and got trapped in orbit. He hated it. And one day, he gave up. He stole a condemned ship, launched himself into space, and drugged himself to sleep. He woke up on Ozero's planet and stepped out into the radiation, knowing exactly how dangerous it was.

At first, he refused to elaborate on why he'd done it, but when pressed by the judge he reluctantly said, "I thought that if I survived, I'd have to find Ozero's family and apologize. If I died, that would be punishment enough—I hoped, anyway. It was just a gamble, like everything else."

But when he was face-to-face with Ozero, all his old instincts kicked back in. If there was one person he wouldn't let kill him, it was this boy whose family he had knowingly ruined, and whose face haunted him in his dreams. He couldn't be that weak.

When asked whether he'd shot himself intentionally, he paused. Finally, he said yes. Did he regret it? No. He would do it again if given the chance.

Ozero listened to his story with a spark of understanding. Understanding, but not pity at first. He tormented himself by wondering what he would've done if he had been in Kem's situation. The fact that he didn't know, and never could know, haunted him until it worked its way into his nightmares, and he could picture himself standing there in his own kitchen with his family's belongings in his arms.

Then he felt a brief moment of pity for Kem. It didn't last long, and it didn't hurt much. But Ozero couldn't stop thinking about it.

Kem was sentenced to life labor on a distant planet. Ozero stood on the dock and watched him get into the spaceship with the other convicted prisoners. That was the ugly side of justice. Kem deserved to suffer, and there was a large part of Ozero that was glad. But another, much smaller part wished Kem had been given a second chance. A chance to overcome the past and change the trajectory of his life. He didn't deserve it, but Ozero still couldn't shake the uncomfortable feeling that he would've wished for forgiveness had their positions been reversed.

*There, but for the grace of God, go I.* He'd read that in a book somewhere, and it seemed appropriate.

Malachi was waiting for him back at the clerics' office. Ozero tried to look unconcerned, but he knew his mental agony was written across his face. Malachi saw it and gave his shoulder an awkward but comforting squeeze.

"You did everything right," he said. "Whether or not Kem decides to become a better person is up to him. You gave him the chance."

Ozero didn't believe he would change. It was pure wishful thinking to believe a person like Kem could reform. Or *should* reform.

But then again, here he was, standing in the clerics' office after years of believing he'd never be better than the little boy checking the locks on his doors with paranoid regularity. He still counted the ceiling tiles while he was working, but now he knew, no matter whether there was an odd or even number of them, that he was more important than they were. And that his fellow clerics would be there to reassure him if he ever forgot.

Hadn't Malachi once told him something . . . something about *how* people could change? Ozero squeezed his eyes shut, trying to remember. It was the day after he'd been rescued from his lonely planet. Malachi and his crewmates were holding a Bible study, which intrigued Ozero, though he didn't really understand what they were trying to achieve.

Malachi had been addressing the group but looked directly at Ozero when he said it: "God can save anyone if they're humble enough to admit they can't save themselves." Then he'd added something about forgiveness being a two-way street. It hadn't seemed important to Ozero until now.

So God was, in some sense, like a perfect version of the clerics, who had saved Ozero's physical form. And if the analogy held—Ozero was beginning to believe that it did—then God could save both him and Kem.

"Are you ready?" asked Malachi, holding the door open expectantly.

"No." Ozero shook his head slowly. "I have to see my family first."

## CHAPTER EIGHT
# FIRST MISSION

He shouldn't have been surprised that they welcomed him back with open arms. For seven years he'd been gone, and he'd hardly thought of them once—they were dead to him because he'd tried to kill all memory of them in his mind. But they had been thinking of him since the day they left, and they didn't want or need to hear his excuses or the speech he'd prepared to apologize for leaving. That didn't matter to them. The moment his mother and sister saw him coming up the sidewalk, they rushed out and squeezed him tight in a bear hug, and that was that.

Ozero had brought them a birthday cake as a peace offering, though it was nobody's birthday. He wondered if it looked anything like the one Kem had stolen from them years ago. Only his mother and sister would know that. They asked him why he'd picked a cake that specifically said "Happy Birthday" when he could've just gotten a blank one, and he told them this was the only one with the flavor he wanted. True, in a sense. It had a flavor of change.

He told them that he'd finally achieved his dream of training to become a cleric, and he told them about Malachi. He didn't say anything about Kem, but he knew they'd find out soon enough. The story was all over the news. What would he say when they asked him why he'd advocated for minimum punishment at the trial? A brief quote from Malachi about forgiveness being a two-way street would have to suffice. He couldn't explain it any better than that yet, but he understood that if *he* wanted to be forgiven for leaving his family, and for holding onto all the bitterness he'd gathered up since he was young, he had to start by forgiving Kem.

Seeing his family disillusioned him from the idea that it was going to be an instant process. The familiar jolt of anger shot through him the moment he opened the refrigerator and saw that his mother and sister had been surviving off a half-empty bottle of milk long past its expiration date. There was still a long way to go, but the choice was made, and now the work had to be done. And Ozero had a feeling that Malachi would help him. "God can save anyone"—Ozero was holding onto that promise.

"Where are we going?" Ozero cast one last glance at the clerics' office ceiling and finalized the number in his mind. Sixteen. A happy even number. Four fours.

"Your first mission by yourself," said Malachi. "You're going back to your little planet. This time, you're going to take people with you. You're going to set up a Federation comms tower there."

He smiled and buttoned up his coat. *Uniform* coat—a uniform he never thought he'd wear.

"Let's go."

*Catastrophe strikes* Transport 80-14 *when passing near an uncharted nebula. One woman, who strove to put her past behind her, is once again thrust into the frontlines in order to survive.*

# THE FATE OF TRANSPORT 80-14

## ALLEN STEADHAM

# CHAPTER ONE
# THE FATE OF *TRANSPORT 80-14*

*"I had fainted, unless I had believed to see the goodness of the LORD
in the land of the living. Wait on the LORD: be of good courage, and
he shall strengthen thine heart: wait, I say, on the LORD."*

Psalm 27:13-14 (KJV)

"**M**om?"

Karen Liviana, the Section Chief of Food Preparation, heard the alarm in her son Darius' voice before she noticed the plates, silverware, and water floating upwards from the sink, mere inches from her. A heartbeat later, she felt her own body rising above the deck plates. Had the chairs and tables from the nearby large mess hall not been magnetically locked to the floor, she and Darius would have sustained serious injuries already. She viewed the floating metal cups, dish rags, and plastic spatula surrounding her with a surreal sense of wonder. Then her military training asserted itself and rapidly quashed her fear.

"The artificial gravity's failed, Darius," she told him in a commanding voice. "Grab something and anchor yourself. I'll find out what's going on."

The trim seventeen-year-old reached forward and took hold of a metal wall ladder as instructed. She found it reassuring to see his alert coffee brown eyes looking at her through his reddish-brown bangs. He was always her first priority. At least he was safe. Now she could focus on equally important matters.

The temperature hadn't dropped any, and she could hear air circulating through the vents in the ceiling. Fortunately, life support was still functional.

She pushed with her legs against the counter she'd been latched onto and drifted weightlessly towards a wall with a communication unit. She endured some glancing impacts from soaring pots, pans, and chopped vegetables as she passed by them. Then she grabbed and held onto the corner of a wall-height storage locker, using muscles honed from years of conditioning. Within sight of her target, she reached across and pounded the "Open Channel" button on the communications unit with her fist.

"Section Chief Liviana to Operations, we've lost gravity on Deck Three," she barked. "What's going on?"

There was a moment of static. The Communications Officer should have responded already, but they hadn't. It took a few more seconds before she heard a response click.

"Chief, this is Commander Ennius. We've encountered an unknown exotic particle concentration emanating from the SNR 1727-41 nebula. It's having a negative impact on multiple systems, including gravity in some areas."

Ennius sounded troubled, which Karen found unusual. August Ennius was second-in-command of *Transport 80-14*. He was an experienced Federated Nations officer. What had him so concerned?

She got her answer when the lighting flickered, and she heard the engines stall.

"Chief, stand by for further instructions," Ennius stated curtly. "I'm heading down to Engineering to assist."

"Copy that, Commander."

Sudden queasiness informed her that the internal stabilizers had gone offline. A heartbeat later, gravity harshly reaffirmed itself and the cold metal deck made a poor cushion for her stout body. There was a sharp pain on the right side of her skull as it struck the floor. She squinted hard in response.

After a few seconds' disorientation, Karen thought she heard her son call out to her and she opened her eyes.

"A-are *you* okay, Darius?"

She felt his hand on her back.

"I'm fine, Mom," he said reassuringly. "Let me help you up, okay?"

"S-Sure."

Darius offered his hand, and she took it. A low groan escaped her lips as she got to her knees and then stood. She had to close her eyes again and lean against him for a moment.

"You're bleeding, Mom!"

She put her hand to her head and felt the slick liquid next to her temple. It stung like a hot poker against her scalp. Even so, it wasn't too serious. She leaned against the kitchen counter and grabbed a nearby dish cloth to stem the flow of blood. Her head started to pound its displeasure at her, but she couldn't afford the distraction, especially now.

Darius rushed to the opposite wall where a standard one-foot by one-foot plastisteel box was attached via magneti-lock. He unsealed and hurriedly brought it to his mother. She massaged derma-gel into her wound and injected some pain reliever into her neck. Within seconds, she felt much better.

Karen briefly hugged her son. Looking at him now, she couldn't help but admire his strong nose, wide smile, and triangular jaw. He looked so much like his father.

Old duty habits and concern for their safety pushed to the surface and forced her to assess their circumstances. She spotted the wall-chrono and verified it was just past 0530 hours.

"Half of the crew was off-duty and probably asleep," Karen said. "I'm sure they're awake now and scrambling to their stations."

"They're probably calling Operations like you did," Darius added.

Karen shook her head. "I don't envy the fourth shift Communications Officer."

"If you were in charge, this probably wouldn't have happened," Darius said under his breath, though Karen could hear him clearly.

That surprised her and she looked at him with concern. "Darius, you shouldn't say things like that. Captain Cicero is an experienced transport officer."

"But you were the Executive Officer on a battlecruiser! You handled all kinds of dangers."

She sighed. "That was twelve years ago, my son. And I took medical retirement so I could raise you after . . . what happened to your father."

"I know, Mom. But you could've —"

"That's enough," she warned, holding up her index finger. "I accept my position in Food Prep, and so should you. It got us free room and board on this ship."

"And if being on this ship gets us killed?" he asked, genuinely worried.

She gently cupped his cheek. "I *won't* let that happen."

A concern began to grow in her thoughts. She still possessed her rank, and she could be called to active status in an emergency. She worried that their present circumstances might qualify.

She and Darius briskly left the kitchen and walked to the adjoining mess hall. She was glad all the metal tables and benches were magneti-locked to the deck. Activating one of the view panels against the far wall let her access visual feeds that surveyed the dusty, gunmetal gray hull on their side of the ship. It was pockmarked from old micrometeorite impacts.

"I don't see any breaches or other signs of distress," Karen said.

"That's good," Darius replied. "What about this nebula? I've never seen anything like it."

The nebula encompassed the rest of their view, even though the ship was passing by its outer edges. Long, thin strands of superheated gases in bright greens, yellows, and reds stretched across light years, roiling and twirling through the cosmos.

"It is unusual. Reminds of a writhing adult kenaworm I once observed protecting its young," she said. "I watched it from a healthy distance through prism lenses on Fenkis Five. The creatures rose up like coiled serpents before lunging at anything they perceived as a threat."

She wondered if this nebula was just as savage in its own way. Noticing the fear in Darius' eyes, even though he didn't voice it, she decided to redirect his attention.

"The transport is coasting on its own inertia," Karen said calmly. "And the hull has been polarized."

"Why does that matter?" he asked. "We're not under attack, are we?"

"No," she replied. "But Commander Ennius mentioned exotic particles. That could mean we've entered a radiation field. Polarizing the hull will hopefully keep us safe until the Chief Engineer and her team can get the engines back online."

Karen looked upward as she heard random tapping noises above her. It prompted her to freeze. The noise was replaced by huge bangs, enough to make the whole transport shudder.

"What is *that*?" he asked.

"It's meteorites," she warned. "Savior help us, we might have entered the outer edges of an asteroid field."

Before Karen could say anything else, the two of them were sharply hurled sideways across the floor as a new impact upended the ship. She and Darius slid into a wall but were fortunate this time. They only had the wind knocked out of them. Immediately, a crisp alarm sounded, followed by an automated voice warning from the computer's artificial intelligence system.

"Condition Gray! Hull breaches in Sections Twelve through Fourteen of Deck Five. Evacuate adjoining sections. Emergency Magneti-Seal has failed in Section Twelve. Magneti-Seal is at twenty-seven percent in Section Thirteen. Magneti-Seal is at eighty-two percent and dropping in Section Fourteen. Repeat: Condition Gray! Evacuate adjoining sections . . . "

Darius looked at his mother with deep concern. "No!"

He looked out towards the view panel and back with sorrowful eyes. Karen knew he was probably thinking about how many of his friends might have passed away. He squeezed his fist tightly.

Karen took a calming breath and straightened the collar of her charcoal-colored uniform. Then she accessed the mess hall communications panel.

"Nineteen crew bio-indicators have gone dark!" Karen exclaimed. "Nineteen out of forty-eight!"

She put her hand against the wall to steady herself. She grew quiet as she whispered, "nineteen souls." Darius looked away for a moment.

"Can we check on some of my friends?" he then asked. "Maybe some of them are all right."

"I'm sorry, but no. We can check on them later. Right now, we have to see how we can help."

Making eye contact with him, she acknowledged his lingering worries and relented some.

"We've both had first aid training. The medical bay isn't far. We can check with Dr. Merab and contact Operations from there to get some answers."

That seemed to appease him, and they exited the mess hall.

Dr. Elizabeth Merab gazed at Commander Drusilla Nona, the salt-and-pepper haired chief engineer of *Transport 80-14*. The sixty-four-year-old was brought into the medical bay with difficulty breathing due to inhaling toxic fumes. She was also suffering debilitating pain from multiple fractures in her right leg.

"Drusilla, you can barely breathe, and that leg can't support your weight yet," Dr. Merab said in an exasperated huff.

"I can manage better than you think, Elizabeth," Drusilla hissed back. "And my team needs me!"

"You're a certified mechanical genius without peer, but you have a chip on your shoulder the size of Dolarus Prime," Dr. Merab insisted.

"What's *that* supposed to mean?"

"You work beyond your shift hours, get far too little rest, and you refuse to change your dietary or exercise habits," the doctor continued.

"I passed my last physical," the engineer retorted.

"I'm still not convinced you didn't use some kind of tech to throw off my bio-scanner."

"If I did, you couldn't *prove* it, doctor," Drusilla said with a smirk.

Not responding to the comment, Dr. Merab added "You even think you can continue to work with these injuries."

"I can!" the engineer asserted.

*Let's put that to a reality check, shall we?* Dr. Merab barely touched her patient's injured leg and then let go. Even so, it caused the older woman to howl in pain.

"Th-that's got to be some kind of ethics violation!" Drusilla wheezed a moment later, furious and now sweating from the discomfort. "Do n-no harm, right?"

Dr. Merab visibly bridled under the accusation but stayed in control of her emotions.

"We've known each other for twenty-five years, Drusilla. I'm hoping a personal appeal will prevail where reason has failed. Barring that, I might have to drug you against your will and face being dragged off in fusion cuffs. That is, if we survive this catastrophe."

"Just try it," Drusilla warned.

Dr. Merab leaned close to the chief engineer and spoke softly but with a firm tone.

"Between your half-scorched lungs and the effects of being tossed into a bulkhead, I would be doing *more* harm letting you go in this condition," Dr. Merab soothed. "Dru, let one of my nurses treat you properly, so you can live to see your husband and grandsons again. I know I want to see my granddaughter on her tenth birthday next month."

Drusilla gave her an angry gaze. "No fair using our grandchildren, Liz." Then she relented. "Fine. Do what you have to do but get me up and walking around as soon as possible!"

Satisfied, Dr. Merab smiled and used a hypo-injector to relieve the engineer of consciousness.

"You have a deal, my friend."

Karen Liviana and her son Darius entered the medical bay and located Dr. Merab. Despite this section being a part of a ten-year-old freighter, Karen was always impressed with how modern it was. She attributed that to its chief medical officer and her illustrious standards. There were ten therapeutic beds, a storehouse of pharmaceuticals, advanced scanning equipment and devices for treatments, not to mentions a planetary library's worth of curative information stored in the transport's computer system. It was also fully staffed daily by three doctors and six nurses across four shifts.

"Dr. Merab, a moment?" Karen said in a respectful tone.

"If you're not sick or wounded, I really *don't* have a moment," the doctor responded gruffly.

"How bad is the situation?" Karen asserted.

Dr. Merab turned around to face Karen and sighed. "If you're asking about the condition of the ship itself, I don't know how bad it is. But we did lose nineteen with that meteor impact, including the captain."

"Captain Cicero is dead?" Karen whispered, her eyes widening. "What about the executive officer?"

Dr. Merab shook her head.

"Commander Ennius helped polarize the hull. He also got several of the crew out of Engineering. But some of the exotic particles entered that section before he could get out. He's dead, too."

Karen closed her eyes and winced in disbelief. Darius visibly paled but stayed quiet. Dr. Merab felt the same as them, but she had to maintain a professional distance from all of it to function. Karen opened her eyes and looked at the doctor.

"Who *is* in command?" Karen asked.

"Normally I'd say the chief engineer, but she'll be out of commission until tomorrow at the earliest," Dr. Merab replied. "And I have my hands full here. You still carry the rank of commander, don't you, Karen? Blue Twelve, if I recall."

Karen looked towards the wounded in the medical bay, then at her son, and back to the doctor. She hesitated to respond.

"That's right," Dr. Merab added with an ironic smile. "*You* are the highest-ranking officer. That means you're in command. Good luck."

Karen pondered how this could happen. Then she reminded herself how small the crew of this freighter was and how drastic their circumstances were. What were the chances, under normal conditions, that this many officers would be unavailable? This was a worst-case scenario in action.

"Dr. Merab, can Darius stay here, if he helps around the medical bay?" Karen asked.

"Does he have any experience treating patients?" Dr. Merab countered.

"I know first aid," Darius chimed in. "I learn quickly and follow instructions well."

Dr. Merab considered the circumstances, soothing her chin with her folded index finger.

"You can shadow my nurses," Dr. Merab replied. "Learn from them, but don't do anything unless they ask you to. They might tell you to check on some of the more stable patients to see if they need anything. Is that okay?"

"Yes, of course!" he answered. "I'll be happy to help."

Then he looked at Karen.

"Mom, please stay safe," he told her. "I'll do what I can here."

Karen gazed at Darius for a long moment. She knew this was the safest place he could be. She was glad he understood, too.

"Say a prayer for us, okay?" She cupped his cheek and smiled reassuringly. "We need it."

With that, Karen gave him a kiss on the forehead and left the medical bay.

Dr. Merab took Darius over to introduce him to Nurse Elena Koto, whom he would be working with.

A man got up from one of the medical beds and walked over behind the doctor. He cleared his throat before speaking. "Excuse me. Doctor?"

It was Lieutenant Lawrence Seleca. She had recently set his left arm with a secure plastisteel brace. He was tall and bald, his skin a toasty caramel brown. He stared at her with pure disbelief on his square face.

"Doctor, how is our *cook* now in command of this vessel?" he asserted.

"Lieutenant, our *cook* also served as executive officer on the *Resolution* twelve years ago," Dr. Merab asserted.

Lt. Seleca looked skeptical. "Twelve years? Then she was in the Battle of Kodos Seven?"

"Yes, she was, Lieutenant," Dr. Merab confirmed. "Her husband died on the *Valiant* in that conflict. My youngest son served under her on the *Resolution*. She's the reason he survived that attack. She's an excellent officer."

*Or at least she was back then. She's changed so much.*

"Are you sure you're not biased because she saved your son, Doctor?" Seleca asked. "She must be pretty rusty after this long."

"Be careful, Lieutenant," Dr. Merab warned. "Whether I have any bias or not, it doesn't change her rank, which I will be happy to certify at your court martial . . . if it comes to that."

Dr. Merab knew that Karen Liviana's actions on the *Resolution* had allowed her son to return home, marry a wonderful woman and have a daughter of his own. The doctor wouldn't tolerate any negativity towards Karen. The poor woman had suffered enough.

There was a moment of understanding between the doctor and the lieutenant.

"She may have the rank, but being so out of practice, she's going to have to earn our respect," Seleca scoffed.

With that, he stormed out of the medical bay.

"I know," the doctor replied wistfully.

As Karen moved through the corridor outside the medical bay, she was rapidly filling with dread. She thought she'd escaped her past, the horrific losses at Kodos Seven, and made a life for herself with Darius at her side. It had been worth accepting medical retirement and giving up the prestige of her position.

She had a simple career in the kitchen, where she could escape her lofty and undeserved reputation as one of the main "heroes" from the Battle of Kodos Seven. She didn't look or feel like the CO of the *Resolution* anymore. Who would look for her on a Federated Nations transport freighter that hauled food and medical supplies to the distant edges of known space? Only Dr. Merab knew she was someone besides Karen the cook or Darius' mother.

Now everything she had accomplished was in jeopardy. Outside of actual combat, this was as bad as things could get. She didn't even know if any distress calls had been made yet. Her identity would be revealed, and the doctor could no longer protect her.

Karen's legs felt increasingly heavy the closer she got to the Operations Deck. She had seen a few crew members running away from the area. Now she was alone in the corridor, only one floor below her destination. She tightly gripped the sides of the ladder which would take her there. But she couldn't lift her legs. No, that wasn't accurate. She just *wasn't* lifting them. She didn't want to do this. Her chokehold on the ladder turned her knuckles white.

In a fit of frustration, Karen shook herself back and forth against the ladder a few times.

Twelve feet straight up and she wouldn't be able to hide anymore. She would have those old responsibilities again. And while she might be able to save lives—perhaps even the ship itself—would she lose who she was, the life she had forged with Darius? She leaned her head forward and let it rest against another of the metal steps. Then she closed her eyes.

"Father, I pray in the name of Your Precious Son, asking You for help and guidance," Karen said softly. "I don't feel worthy or ready. I know I have my duty, but I don't know how to carry it out. Please bless me with Your wisdom and mercy. Show me how to lead these people. They have no one else. I will lean and depend on You alone. Please protect those who are still in danger at this very moment. Show me how to help them, if it's Your will. I pray and ask everything in Jesus' name. Amen."

In that moment, she knew she would be all right. They would make it out of this alive. She just had to help them hold on until help arrived. And somehow, she knew it *would* arrive. In her thoughts, she thanked God with all her heart.

And then, tightening her grip on the ladder once more, she pulled herself up to a standing position and ascended to the Operations Deck.

# CHAPTER TWO

## TWELVE YEARS AGO. BATTLE CRUISER *RESOLUTION* IN ORBIT OVER KODOS SEVEN.

Commander Karen Liviana ignored the searing pain from her exposed and burned left shoulder and kept her eyes on the viewing screen in front of her. Her long, disheveled ginger-red hair was partially obstructing her view, but she could see enough. The Alkieh warship *Ymdar* was unscathed before them. It had fired only seconds before without warning. That unexpected—and cowardly, in Liviana's opinion—first strike had breached their hull mid-ship, disabled the *Resolution*'s Jump Drive, and murdered one-third of the six-hundred-and-twenty-member crew. The air was acrid from short-circuited wiring and debris-blocked ventilation ducts. The captain was being taken to Medical, mortally injured from shrapnel. She didn't expect him to survive. Without Jump Drive, they couldn't run. And the rest of the fleet was engaged with their Alkieh counterparts, so the *Resolution* was on its own. They had to fight. But she knew so little about their enemy's technology, it made tactical response challenging at best.

"The captain of the *Ymdar* is offering us two options, Commander: honorable surrender or honorable death by combat. They have given us five minutes to respond."

She turned her head to look at the burly man who spoke, Tactical Officer Lieutenant Moses Plinius, at the weapons console behind her.

"How generous," Liviana said in disgust. "Is the hull polarized now?"

"Yes, Commander, but only at sixty-eight percent effectiveness," he replied. "However, weapons batteries are fully charged and ready, as are proton warheads."

"Good," Liviana said. Then she punched her fist down on the captain's chair communications panel. "Engineering: Chief, I need a status report."

The background noises, including the hissing of broken conduits and crackling from damaged machinery, made it difficult to hear Lieutenant Commander Maximillian Flavius. When Liviana asked him to repeat what he said, he responded much louder in his deep, gravelly voice.

"Commander, it's bad! I can give you full speed now, but no long-range jumps."

"Understood, Chief."

"Whatever you do, you'll have to do it fast. We'll have full power for about fifteen more minutes. Then we're on backup only, and you know what that means."

She knew. Backup power would only keep life support, lights, and station-keeping thrusters functional. If the enemy still had weapons, they'd be as good as dead.

Then an idea popped into her mind.

"What about micro-jumps?" she asked the engineer. "Can you jump us *into* the Alkieh vessel?"

There was a long moment's silence from the chief engineer.

"Yes, Commander," the engineer stressed. "In our current state, we can execute one micro-jump."

"I need two, Chief: one to get us there and one to get away," Liviana ordered. "Just do it."

If they didn't make two jumps, Liviana knew this was going to be a suicide run. And she owed the crew more than that.

A shorter silence followed.

"Yes, Commander," the engineer conceded. "I'll tie in the backups. That will give us enough power for two micro-jumps."

"Make it happen, Chief," Liviana added.

She appraised the Alkieh vessel before her on the screen. It had a sleek, almost glistening, turquoise-colored hull. It was smaller than the *Resolution*. It reminded her of a falcon. But in the *Resolution*'s current state, the *Ymdar* was faster and better armed. She couldn't underestimate them.

"The enemy is waiting for our response to either surrender or fight," the commander said with a grim smile. "Let's give them one. Helm, full speed the way we came."

"Yes, Commander," the helmsman responded. "Heading out of the system at full speed."

Liviana could feel the movement of the ship. The engines were being pushed beyond their current capacity. The sickly feeling in her stomach confirmed that the stabilizers were straining to compensate. But Liviana knew what the *Resolution* was capable of.

The helmsman, Lieutenant Luke Merab, was already impressing her with his evasive maneuvering of the ship, but she knew that couldn't last. The *Ymdar* would lock onto them at any second. Any more damage could compromise this whole plan.

"Tactical, I need full hull polarization for the next thirty seconds. Arm four proton warheads. Set them for manual release, five-second detonation delay," Liviana demanded.

"Yes, Commander," Plinius replied.

That would give them the best chance of surviving the initial impact, remaining functional to carry out the rest of her plan.

It was a desperate idea, she thought, given the reduction in the *Resolution*'s propulsion capabilities. What she was considering was beyond foolhardy. Actually, it would be considered insane by other commanders. But it was the only move the enemy couldn't possibly anticipate or counter.

"As soon as we complete Jump One, drop the warheads!" Liviana shouted. "Engineering, I need that first jump now! Immediate Jump Two on impact!"

The next four seconds were complete chaos.

The familiar sensation of a gradual engine build-up and forward momentum surge was replaced with a savage blink, explosions, and screams. Metal was grinding against metal. Then there was a succession of sounds as the proton warheads exited their deployment tubes: *Thunk, Thunk, Thunk, Thunk.* By now, they were locked to the *Ymdar*'s hull. Another blink was followed by a whirlwind of motion, noise, and pain.

Liviana didn't know how long she'd been unconscious. Barely able to open her eyes, she knew her back was on the deck now. Her hazy vision registered the dim emergency lights flickering on the ceiling. Smoke from burning consoles and flesh stung her nostrils. When she eventually managed to roll to one side, a blinding pain in her left arm let her know it had been dislocated. She could tell she had at least one cracked or broken rib. But she was alive.

Now, she had to somehow stand up and check on her crew. Despite her body's protestations and eschewing the use of her left arm, she soon made her way to the helmsman and tactical officer near the front of the operations deck. Merab was breathing, though he had nasty gashes on his forehead and right arm. Plinius was clearly dead. His stolid eyes were still open, and his neck was at an unnatural angle. She silently closed his eyelids. Then she helped Merab sit up. After that, she verified that the communications officer, Lieutenant Chloe Saturna, was alive but badly injured. She had suffered burns to the right side of her body. She told the commander she was numb from the chest down, indicating a spinal injury. Liviana thought Saturna needed to be in the medical bay already. She regretted she couldn't take the woman there herself, but duty and her own injuries wouldn't allow it.

Liviana soon discovered their attack on the Alkieh ship had been devastatingly successful. Miraculously, the viewing screen was still operational, blurring now and then with static. One proton warhead was powerful enough to disable a ship that size. They had used four. In the space before them, all that remained of the vessel was a cloud of debris and the floating fragments from what had been more than three hundred Alkieh soldiers.

"Merab, pull up short-range sensors, if we still have them," Liviana commanded. "How is the ship? And I want to know how the rest of the battle is going."

The twenty-something Helmsman limped to the sensor console to his left. After a few commands brought up the needed information, he turned his head to face Liviana.

"The ship is mostly intact and drifting, Commander. Life support is at sixty percent and main power is offline. Backups are at forty-five percent," he reported. "One hundred and sixty-three survivors."

Liviana felt a chill run throughout her body at that revelation. Her orders had caused the loss of two hundred and sixty lives. *Her* actions. She had condemned more of her crew to death than the enemy. She would have to bear that burden the rest of her days.

"The battle is mostly over, Commander," the helmsman added.

The *Resolution* was part of a fleet of twenty FNS battle cruisers that had been publicly sent to this location. However, another fleet, comprised of two hundred battle cruisers and destroyers, had been secretly deployed directly to the Alkieh homeworld to force the enemy's surrender.

The Alkieh were a xenophobic species whose empire spanned three star systems but they had stayed within their own borders for well over a century. Their leader, Ub'ieltomach, had made a treaty with the Federated Nations upon their initial contact. But he had died recently and one of his offspring, Ul'iksakeh, had replaced him. The new emperor sent out forces to conquer outlying worlds for the Alkieh Empire. And more than a few of those planets were in Federated Nations space.

Since then, there had been numerous skirmishes to retake those worlds. However, the Alkieh had developed new and powerful technologies during their isolation. The Federated Nations had suffered several crushing defeats in the last year, resulting in a declaration of war and a substantial increase in forces dedicated to repelling the Alkieh invaders. All of those events had led to this final conflict above the disputed world of Kodos Seven.

The FNS' top commanders had mapped the locations of all Alkieh ship deployments. They were aware that their enemy had spread their forces too thin to adequately protect their enlarged territory and their homeworld at the same time.

But the fleet at Kodos Seven had been critical to the Commanders' plans. If the Alkieh stayed focused on the forces near that world, they would never see the main fleet until it was too late.

"The FNS fleet decimated the Alkieh forces at their homeworld. The current Alkieh battle group has been reduced by half. Those ships are currently in retreat."

"How is our fleet?"

"Intact, Commander. Most sustained damage but are operational. Our ship and the *Pyrrhus* are disabled. We lost only four out of twenty vessels," he reported. "The *Polaris*, the *Xerxes*, the *Bayonet*, and . . . the *Valiant*."

The FNS *Valiant*. Her husband's ship. He was one of the engineers. The loss was too much, too sudden. She couldn't face it yet. Instead, she buried herself in her duty a moment longer.

She contacted the medical bay from a communications panel and requested assistance for the surviving Operations officers. Her own injuries would have to wait. Besides, they would remind her she was still alive . . . and that Julius Liviana wasn't. Her husband, the father of their son. The man who had won her whole heart.

She stifled her own feelings then, shoved them so far down that they wouldn't interfere until after she got her crew safely home. They deserved that much for following her orders.

Commander Liviana and the other wounded from the *Resolution* were taken to the Nexus 228 medical facility in orbit of Kodos

Prime. Liviana had three broken ribs, burns, and a dislocated arm. By the time they arrived, Ensign Merab was almost fully healed. His mother, Dr. Elizabeth Merab, was stationed at Nexus 228. The doctor aided in Liviana's treatment and took that time to get to know her. She had been the one who had advised Liviana to take medical retirement in order to raise Darius and heal from her losses.

They had been close ever since. Liviana knew the doctor considered her and her son family.

# CHAPTER THREE

## THE PRESENT. *TRANSPORT 80-14* NEAR THE SNR 1727-41 NEBULA.

Operations was only being manned by two people: the communications officer, Lieutenant Muriel Boudica, and a Security Officer, Ensign Randall Nechtan. Boudica was a slim woman in her mid-twenties who had signed up with the freighter eighteen months ago. She was shy and had been discretely pursuing a relationship with Commander Ennius.

Right now, Karen thought poor Muriel looked like she had aged twenty years. She could empathize. Muriel had lost the love of her life today and was still trying to function. Stress lines had already etched themselves below her sleep-deprived eyes and across her brow. Her sandy blonde hair was as frazzled as her nerves. She could see the woman switching between communications channels at lightning speed, answering one question before acknowledging a damage report and making an attempt to send a distress call. All Muriel got from the emergency channel was static, no matter how many times she tried.

Karen only watched her for a moment, not wanting to give the woman a heart attack by announcing her presence. Finally, Muriel screamed "I give up!" and slammed her fists on the console before resting her head on it. Ensign Nechtan continued to stand at parade rest near the back of Operations, silent and the epitome of professional.

"Muriel? I'm sorry to interrupt," Karen eventually said.

Muriel lifted her head and seemed unclear whether the other voice was real. She craned her neck to verify.

"Karen?" she said, disoriented. "Why are you here?"

Karen wanted to be as reassuring as possible.

"With the loss of Command Staff in Operations, I was needed," Karen replied softly.

Muriel stared at her in confusion for a couple of seconds.

"Well, as much as I'd love for you to make some sandwiches about now, I don't think that's going to help get us out of this."

Karen half-smiled at Muriel's gallows humor. But it was time to get down to business.

"I take it long-range communications are down?" she asked Muriel.

Muriel straightened her posture and attempted to smooth her hair back to recollect herself.

"Uh, yeah. I've been trying to send a distress call, but the array must have been damaged."

Karen nodded then considered something else.

"All FNS vessels are equipped with disaster buoys, aren't they?"

The younger woman thought about it. "You're right! Wait, how'd you know that?"

"Program the distress call into a disaster buoy and launch it away from the nebula," Karen instructed. "Activate its short-range Jump Drive to get it closer to a relay satellite. We'll receive a faster response that way."

"That's a good plan," Muriel acknowledged, taken aback by the suggestion.

Muriel pressed several buttons and then Karen felt a quick shudder from the ship. On the viewing screen, Karen watched the distress buoy pull ahead of the ship by perhaps a hundred meters. Its small rectangular jump drive glowed bright blue as it came online and the buoy blinked out of view a moment later.

"The disaster beacon is now a sector away and transmitting," Muriel reported. "But I still don't know how you know all this."

"Long story," Karen told her. "Do we still have ship-wide intercast?"

Muriel just looked at her stupefied. "Yes. Why?"

Karen knew how her next statement would sound, but she made it anyway.

"Patch me through, ship-wide, Muriel."

"Are you crazy?" Muriel exclaimed. "Do you know the kind of trouble you and I will get in for an unauthorized ship-wide broadcast?"

Karen understood Muriel's apprehension, but she didn't have time to explain. She moved the stunned Communications Officer aside.

"Please trust me right now," Karen told Muriel.

Karen typed in the commands herself. A second later, a short chime sounded all over the transport, heralding an important announcement from Operations.

"Attention, crew of *Transport 80-14*, this is a Priority Alpha Communication. For the last five years, you have known me as Karen Liviana, section chief of food preparation," she began. "But I also hold the active rank of commander, Classification Blue Twelve. My authorization is Pi-One-One-Zero. I have taken command of this vessel under Article Thirteen of Regulation Ten-A, which dictates that when all senior officers have been killed or incapacitated, the next highest-ranking officer should assume command.

"I need the chief medical officer, the chief of security, and every surviving engineer to report to the operations deck immediately," she continued. "Everyone else, seek shelter in the designated safe zones on Decks Two, Three, and Four. Security personnel, you will verify compliance with these orders. Liviana out."

By the time Karen finished, Muriel was as wide-eyed as any animal mounted on a wall.

"Lieutenant Boudica, assist me in patching critical systems to terminals here in Operations," Karen ordered.

"Y-Yes, Commander," Muriel stammered.

By the time they completed the work, three men and two women had climbed the ladder to enter the deck. She recognized the engineers from their previous visits to the mess hall. Lieutenant Seleca was joined by Ensign Cade Quintus, a hulking figure of a man with square glasses and blond hair. Next to him was Ensign Antonia Varinia. She was twenty-six years old, had long wavy black hair and eyes the deepest shade of emerald.

Dr. Merab was now present, looking ready to assist. Beside her was the short and brawny security chief, Lieutenant Nikolai Zakhar. He was in his mid-thirties, clean-shaven, with very close-cropped golden-brown hair.

Cade spoke first. "Commander, what's going on?"

Karen hardened her expression as she returned his gaze. "I need to know what this ship can still do, Ensign," she replied. Then she turned her attention to Seleca and Varinia. "Using these consoles, how fast can you three engineers determine engine status, danger from the asteroid field, and how soon help might arrive? A disaster buoy was just launched and is transmitting a distress call from one sector away."

Antonia and Seleca visibly bristled at Karen's new demeanor, but Cade accepted it.

"Commander, permission to speak freely?" Seleca asked Karen.

She didn't want to indulge him, but she also wanted to engender trust. She nodded. "Go ahead, Lieutenant."

"Twenty-two escape capsules are currently functional. I recommend we evacuate as many crew as we can. We should follow that disaster buoy," Seleca suggested.

Antonia slowly nodded and Cade pondered the suggestion. The doctor looked at Seleca with irritation and Zakhar kept a straight face.

Karen suppressed her own aggravation and suppressed a sigh.

"First of all, those weren't my orders," Karen said stiffly. "Secondly, the escape capsules have no Jump Drives or hull polarization. The gravity pull from the asteroid field varies by the size of the rocks out there. Without being a significant distance away, we would risk most of the capsules being pulled into the field. If they aren't crushed by the asteroids, their occupants would die from the radiation."

Seleca's expression cemented.

"Our odds for dying seem the same either way. If we stay with the ship, we die," he continued. "But if we—"

"That's enough, Lieutenant!"

Seleca visibly chafed at Karen's rebuke. She'd seen this kind of behavior before: the strain on inexperienced officers facing dire circumstances for the first time.

"We have enough escape capsules to evacuate eighty percent of the crew, maybe more!" Seleca insisted.

"Lieutenant, you're relieved," Karen directed. "Please go to one of the designated—"

Seleca's fear suddenly turned to anger and resentment. He pulled a mini-pistol from his belt with his right hand and lunged forward to grab Karen. She pulled away, suppressing a gasp. Her eyes quickly narrowed.

"Drop it, Lieutenant!" The Security Chief had already trained his own pistol on Seleca. Karen knew he was looking for any opening that could stop Seleca while preserving her life. Zakhar wouldn't hesitate to kill the man.

Seleca must have been aware of that, too. Less than two feet from Karen, he kept his weapon focused on her face, his index finger ready to pull the trigger. She had assumed a mask of calm and her eyes never left his.

"Put the weapon down, Lieutenant," she said coolly.

Seleca took a quick glance at Zakhar, then returned his attention to Karen.

"Look, we're going! I've got it all worked out," Seleca demanded. "You can come with us or you can stay. I don't care—"

The Lieutenant had been so focused on Karen and Zakhar that he didn't notice Dr. Merab position herself behind him until she put a hypo-injector to his neck. After a quick clicking sound from the device, Seleca's eyes rolled back, and he collapsed to the floor unconscious.

"I had a feeling he'd cause trouble," the doctor said, looking down at him.

Karen gave her a grateful nod.

Dr. Merab walked over to Chief Zakhar and smiled. "Our unhinged mutineer will be asleep for the next twelve hours."

"Acknowledged, Doctor," Zakhar said. Then he turned his attention to his fellow Security Officer. "Ensign Nechtan, you and I will relocate Lieutenant Seleca to the brig."

"Yes, Lieutenant."

Zakhar and Nechtan each took one of Seleca's arms and dragged the unconscious man away.

Karen sighed, leaning against the Captain's chair.

"I wish he hadn't done that," she said. "He's not a bad officer. He just—"

"Pardon me, Commander," Dr. Merab interjected. "But the man just insulted and threatened a superior officer with force."

Karen didn't have any more time to indulge the doctor's vindictive nature.

She turned to face Antonia and Cade. "Can I depend on you two to follow my orders?"

Antonia still looked completely astonished. She looked towards the exit. Had she identified that much with Seleca's intentions? Cade, on the other hand, appeared pleased and maybe relieved.

"You can depend on me, Commander," Cade said.

Karen waited on Antonia, who still seemed conflicted. Would it be better to relieve the ensign of duty now?

"I will do what I can . . . Commander," Antonia finally said.

"You will follow *all* my orders, whether you agree with them or not," Karen demanded.

"Yes, Commander," she replied.

"Then get me the information I requested."

Ten minutes later, the two engineers stood in front of Karen at attention and ready to give their reports.

"Commander, the good news is that the ship's inertia is causing it to continue drifting away from the asteroid field," Antonia said. "The bad news is that there's one large planetoid ahead that could pull us into another cluster. That area also appears to be dense in the exotic particles we detected before."

Karen pondered that information a moment. "Thank you, Ensign Varinia. What about our engines, Ensign Quintus?"

Cade smiled, eager to relay his information. "I have more good news, Commander. There wasn't very much physical damage from the earlier impacts. The Jump Drive is offline and would take about four hours to repair if we had a full engineering detachment. Since it's just me and Ensign Varinia, I don't know how feasible that is. I do believe we can restore full-speed capability to the fusion core. There's just one problem."

Cade handed his palm-sized device to Antonia for her opinion. She studied its findings and nodded morosely. Then she returned her gaze to Karen.

"One component needs to be bypassed to get the fusion core back online," Antonia expressed. "Either Ensign Quintus or I could do the work. Normally, it would take maybe fifteen minutes."

Karen picked up on Antonia's underlying concern.

"What makes this abnormal?" Karen asked her.

"The engine component is adjacent to Main Engineering. They share several conduits and crawlspaces," Antonia replied. "And Main Engineering is still contaminated with exotic particles."

Karen's jaw started to drop, but she mastered her emotions. Here it was, the type of command decision she had been dreading. It was literally staring her in the face. The anxiety was already making her

THE FATE OF TRANSPORT 80-14     159

stomach churn. She tried to stifle her emotions like she had in the past, but it was more difficult this time.

*They're almost young enough to be my kids.*

"I see. What are our chances of being pulled in by the planetoid?" she asked Antonia with some trepidation.

"Quite high, Commander," she answered. "A seventy percent chance or better within the next three hours."

Karen turned to Cade. "Do you concur, Ensign?"

"I do, Commander," he said.

Karen wanted to pace. Actually, she wanted to be anywhere but here.

"And what are the chances of firing up the engines and getting us to a safe distance if . . . someone does the work near the fusion core?"

"Virtually one hundred percent, Commander," Antonia reported. Cade nodded his assent.

Karen had to force herself to breathe in and out slowly to remain calm.

"Would the protection of an environmental suit help your chances of survival?" Karen asked, figuratively grasping at straws. "Or some kind of inoculation from the doctor?"

Dr. Merab shook her head at the Commander.

"It might buy them a few extra minutes to get their work done, but these are unknown exotic particles emitting a unique and especially harmful radiation," Dr. Merab said. "I don't have anything to inoculate them with. And even in a protective environmental suit, I estimate irreversible exposure in less than ten minutes and death within a day."

Karen frowned, considering if there was any alternative. She could only think of one.

"Can the work be done by someone other than an engineer?" Karen asked them.

That surprised and confused both junior officers. They looked at each other with puzzlement before returning their attention to their commander.

"Why would you want someone else to do the work?" Cade asked. "Who did you have in mind?"

"Me," Karen answered. "When I was on the *Resolution*, I had to do more than a few engine repairs and tune ups. Is it something I could do?"

Cade stepped forward a bit, appearing very concerned.

"With all due respect, Commander, I would have to say no," he said. "This may just be a freighter, but fusion core engines have had several significant upgrades over the last decade. I could not, in good conscience, recommend for anyone without current training to operate or repair them. It would reduce our chances by more than half, perhaps undermine them altogether."

"I'm forced to agree with Ensign Quintus, Commander," Antonia said earnestly.

Karen turned away from the doctor and engineers. She wasn't sure she could repress her reaction and wanted to retain her composure. She squinted.

*Are these the only options? Savior, please, I beg You: show me a third alternative!*

Knowing the time to decide was now, she honestly didn't know what to do. She stalled for a few more seconds.

"I've read both of your service records. You're both more than qualified to do this work," Karen said. "And now, I have to decide which of you to send."

She didn't have to add "to your death."

Karen allowed herself a long sigh.

"This is very troubling to me," she admitted. "If I thought Seleca's idea had any merit, I'd still consider it."

She sat down in the captain's chair. She rested her hands in her lap. "I don't miss this chair. Or the grief that comes with it."

"Is there a problem, Commander?" Antonia asked.

"Cade and the doctor know this, but you and I haven't had too many conversations, Ensign Varinia," Karen said. "I'm a Christian now and a pacifist. I've given control of my life to God. Yet now, control has been given to me—of this vessel and crew."

She stood, taking a few steps away from the others before stopping and turning around. She looked more resolute.

"The military can only function through its command structure," Karen continued. "Everyone reports and answers to their superior officer. And I'm looking at God as my Commanding Officer, waiting on Him for instructions."

The ensigns and doctor reflected a silent awkwardness in their stances. They most likely did not expect this sudden sharing from the commander.

Before Karen could say anything else, there was a tremendous crash. The ship tilted one-hundred and sixty degrees forward. She heard her three fellow officers cry out in distress. Any personnel or equipment not magneti-sealed to the deck went flying. That included Karen, who was hurled towards one of the computer consoles. She felt her right arm break where it impacted above the elbow, and her forehead smacked into an unforgiving surface, almost robbing her of consciousness. A second later, the numbness in her head was replaced by a white-hot sensation of her chest colliding with the floor. She didn't know how anyone else was doing. She didn't even know how she was doing. Each breath felt like daggers stabbing her lungs. She couldn't open her eyes, but she could still hear.

"Condition Gray! Hull breaches in Sections Two and Three, Deck Four," the computer alerted. "Evacuate adjoining sections. Emergency Magneti-Seal failure in Section Two. Condition Gray!"

Moments later, she heard the muffled sounds of someone running across the deck. They kneeled down beside her.

"Commander!" Dr. Merab said. She sounded very worried.

But the doctor was interrupted by a low rumbling throughout the freighter that quickly rose in volume and intensity. It wasn't another impact; it was something else. The ship jolted occasionally.

"Someone go fix that engine!" Dr. Merab shouted.

"I'll do it, Doctor!" Antonia bellowed in response. "Quintus, start the engines after I'm done! Get us *out* of here!"

"Roger that!" Cade yelled.

Just then, Karen's pain overwhelmed her, and she lost consciousness.

# CHAPTER FOUR

## TWO DAYS LATER. *FNS INTREPID* (EXPLORATION CLASS). TRAVELING AWAY FROM THE SNR 1727-41 NEBULA.

Karen had drifted between sleeping and being semi-awake until now, occasionally feeling bouts of pain and the soothing release caused by medication. Feeling more aware, she blinked several times and tried to focus her eyes. She was in a Medical Bay, but not the one she was used to.

"Mom?"

She turned her head and was surprised at how sore she was. It was worth the effort to see Darius' handsome young face. His expression was a mixture of concern and delight.

"Darius," Karen said, her voice weak.

"You were hurt, Mom, but Dr. Merab says you're gonna be all right."

Karen relaxed back into the pillow and closed her eyes.

"What happened?" she asked.

"Well, I see my star patient has regained consciousness," Dr. Merab interjected.

Karen opened her eyes long enough to see the doctor's relieved expression. Elizabeth Merab looked spent. She wondered how long it had been since the doctor had slept.

"You tried to check out on me once or twice, but I wouldn't let you," Dr. Merab said. "You're in the *Intrepid*'s Medical Bay."

"When . . . did they get to us?" Karen asked.

"About eighteen hours after you had Muriel send that distress call. The freighter's in tow."

"H-How many did we lose, Elizabeth?"

The doctor gave her a reassuring smile.

"Don't worry about that. You just get some more rest."

Karen didn't have much choice in that, as she lost consciousness again.

The next morning, Karen woke again, this time she had more energy. The wall-chrono's digital display informed her it was nearly 0630 hours. She hoped her son was getting some sleep. She recalled that Dr. Merab had said they were on the *Intrepid*.

Was *Transport 80-14* salvageable, she considered. If it wasn't, she and her son would have to find a new ship, a new home. Or was she getting ahead of herself? How was the crew? How bad were her own injuries?

Karen tried to sit up. That was when she realized her right arm was in a plastisteel brace. Her chest was sore, but not as badly as before. Pain medication was dulling her senses and reflexes.

A brawny blonde-haired nurse rushed over to steady Karen and help her lay back down.

"Commander, you're in no condition t'move about," the nurse told her. She had a strong Caledon Colony accent and sounded young to

Karen. "I can angle the med-bed t'make you more comfortable, let you watch the vid-feeds. How's that sound?"

"Thank you." Karen acceded. "I need to speak to Dr. Merab, please."

Dr. Merab came by an hour later. Darius arrived within minutes after that. By then, Karen was feeling more awake.

"How's my patient?" the doctor asked.

"Isn't this how we met, Elizabeth?" Karen replied.

The doctor nodded. "This does have kind of a deja vu feel, doesn't it?"

"I'm feeling better today," Karen said. "Can you bring me up to speed on everything?"

The doctor pulled one of the metal chairs closer to Karen's bed and sat down. Darius was already sitting in one.

"Sure, Karen," the doctor replied. "You were injured when some more asteroid fragments hit the ship. We didn't know it at the time, but something caused the gravitational forces in that region of space to temporarily increase."

"Something? Do we know now what caused it?" Karen asked.

Dr. Merab shook her head.

"That's why the *Intrepid* was sent in," she answered Karen. "Their science team downloaded *80-14*'s sensor logs, but their Science Officer, Lieutenant Yanis, said it could take months or longer to interpret the data."

That surprised Karen. "Why so long?"

Dr. Merab shrugged. "How should I know? I studied medicine, not the stars. Anyway, Ensigns Varinia and Quintus only had scrapes and bruises. But you nearly shattered your right arm and suffered a concussion from the first impact. You punctured a lung and broke three ribs when you hit the floor. I've got a lot more gray hairs now, thanks to you. But it's a good thing you have such a thick skull, Karen."

She chuckled in response. But something didn't quite add up to Karen.

"Did the *Intrepid* arrive early? The engineers didn't have to make the repairs?" she asked.

"No. Ensign Varinia made the engine repairs and Ensign Quintus got us to full speed," the doctor replied. "That's how we were able to get to the *Intrepid* when we did."

Karen's heart sank. "Then Antonia is dead?"

Karen heard someone enter the medical bay but couldn't turn her head to see who it was. The person walked closer.

"No, Commander." She could see now that it was Antonia. With arms folded at her waist, she smiled at Karen. "I'm still here."

Karen felt a joy spring up within her. "I'm so glad you're safe, Ensign!".

"Thank you, Commander. It was a surprise to me as well."

"Finally," Dr. Merab interjected. "Someone who can explain the science!"

Antonia laughed at that. Karen wasn't used to seeing the young woman so at ease. What had happened?

"I'll explain what I can," the ensign said. "We still don't know what caused the gravitational shift, but we do know a lot more about the asteroids in the area."

"What did you learn?" Karen inquired.

"The change in gravity caused them to smash into each other . . . and us," Antonia shared. "It exposed their cores, which are comprised of substances as unique as the nebula's exotic particles—with one crucial difference."

Karen nodded for her to continue.

"The substances in the asteroid cores *absorb* the exotic particles, essentially cancelling them out," Antonia added. "Before the last impact, they had actually been decontaminating our freighter, though we didn't know it. By the time I started the repairs, Engineering and the surrounding areas of the ship were at a low enough particle density that my environmental suit fully protected me. Ensign Quintus did his part and now we're here."

Dr. Merab let out a long sigh.

"A miracle," she said. "That's what it is."

"Some people say miracles are just science that hasn't been explained yet," Antonia added.

Dr. Merab crossed her arms and looked at the young ensign askance.

"Look, Ensign, you call it what you want," the doctor said. "I'm no Christian, but even I know a miracle when I see it. And you're still breathing because of one. So are twenty-five others."

That filled Karen with new concern.

"Who did we lose?" she asked the doctor.

"Camillus, Jovian, and Itamar," Dr. Merab answered wistfully. "The injuries they sustained in the original impact were too severe."

Karen nodded. "I know you did all you could."

Dr. Merab gave Karen a bittersweet smile. "I'll check back on you in a bit. We have fourteen others from *80-14* recovering here, so I've been helping Dr. Sarcophagus."

"You just like the work," Karen jested.

Dr. Merab's mood lightened, and she shrugged before heading into another room. Ensign Varinia stepped closer to Karen's bedside.

"I've been coming by to check on you, but this is the first time you've been awake, Commander," Antonia said. "I'm glad you're doing better. If I can be of any help, to you or your son, let me know."

"Thank you, Ensign," Karen replied. "I will."

The ensign walked out of the medical bay. Darius patted his mother's left arm.

"Looks like you finally made friends with her, Mom," he said.

"I guess so, huh?"

Darius let his mother know what he had learned: *Transport 80-14* would undergo full repairs and be inspected to determine its space-worthiness within four or five weeks.

"Dr. Merab said your recuperation will take a couple more weeks," Darius told her.

She took her son's hand in hers. "Sounds like we may have some free time then. Want to go on a vacation?"

He grinned at that. "I sure would, Mom! What did you have in mind?"

"I went to the academy with the *Intrepid*'s Commanding Officer, Captain Hunter. I might be able to talk him into lending us a Jump Craft or maybe dropping us off at Iyago Nine?"

Darius's eyes became saucer-like as he smiled.

"I heard that world has two-mile high waterfalls and the best nature preserve in the region!" he exclaimed.

Karen nodded. "So that's a yes, then?"

"Definitely!"

Darius stayed with her another couple of hours before she insisted he get lunch and socialize with others. She knew he'd be back later, and she loved him for it.

She spent some time in prayer. She studied scriptures on her bedside computer console, meditating over them and her recent circumstances. She discovered more and more reasons to be thankful to God.

She had asked for His intervention and she believed that was exactly what had happened. Not only had He changed the laws of physics to affect local gravity, but He had used it to expose the asteroids' cores and decontaminate the ship. She knew that God had made it possible for Ensign Varinia to do her job without sacrificing her life.

Karen didn't have to make the life-or-death decision that came with Command this time. God had relieved her of that burden, saving her crew and ship. Now that the crisis was over, she didn't have to remain an active Commander anymore. God had allowed her to go back to doing what she loved, being a cook and Darius' Mom.

And she would forever be grateful.

*When Nexus 721 is bombarded by exotic particles from a nearby nebula, Cleric Malachi Jones is sent to assess the situation and collect survivors. Yet he's presented with an impossible choice—one that no cleric has ever had to face.*

# THE INTERVIEW OF MALACHI JONES

## DAPHNE SELF

# CHAPTER ONE
# DEATH COMES MARCHING

They were heard long before I saw them. The dreaded *thump-thump* of marching combat boots. *Thump-thump.*

Memories clawed their way from the back of my mind at the sound; memories I had strove to bury and destroy, but that was the way of memories, not allowing themselves to be shunted aside as forgotten pieces of furniture or miscellaneous items of unimportance.

For years I had known the time would come, but I had hoped it wouldn't have come so soon.

I threw another shovel load of broken terrain and rock into the cart behind me. *Thump-thump. Thump-thump.* The boots closed in on my section of the mining tunnel.

Another load hit the cart and rocked it to the side, almost off its tracks. *Thump.*

Shovels stilled. Rocks settled. Broken terrain trickled down the sides of the tunnel. Dust plumed around my feet, and I scooped another load onto the shovel head.

I cast the contents into the cart and glanced at the man to my left. My gaze settled on his lapel. Two yellow slashes. Cleric third grade of Gamma Order.

Dread was an infant compared to what soaked into my heart. Was it some folly of an idea that I had to believe that what I did would not invoke the wrath of the Cleric? Did I actually believe that the Federated Nations would lobby for my life?

Yeah, I actually did believe that. What I fool I had been.

I leaned against my shovel. "Cleric?"

Dust floated and then clung to the black outfits. It'd be hard to scrub the moon dust from that material. That was my only consolation for what was about to happen.

He pulled a film-plast from his jacket, unrolled it, held it in front of him, and activated the screen, his movements precise. His eyes flicked back and forth from the representation on the screen to me and then back again. Several times it occurred before he spoke.

"Malachi Jones. Please confirm your name, rank, and designation."

I let the shovel fall to the ground. Around him the other four officers stepped back, hands on trigger guards, and watched warily. A laugh wanted to escape from me, but I only sighed.

Those days that I instilled fear were long gone. Couldn't they see that? Did they expect me to magically produce exploding rocks or cast irradiated moon dirt their way that they would need a defense against?

"Malachi Jones. I repeat, please confirm your name, rank, and designation." The film-plast never wavered. His eyes stared hard into mine.

I almost wanted to say to him, *Nope. Thomas Barclay. Fourth shift tunnel three miner. Classification, red zero.* A load of good that would have been since he held my service record in his hands. Seven years of running, of beard growth, of bleaching and dyeing, and scarification wouldn't change the fact that they found me.

He motioned the four closer. They stepped forward with rifles raised.

I spoke before he could give me the courtesy of the third and final commandment before summary judgement. "Malachi Jones. Cleric First Grade, White Judgement First Class, Zed Order."

It was a distinct pleasure, albeit short lived, to see the men nervously take a half step back with their rifles primed. I held out my hands, wrist together. Better to go peacefully than to let them use force. They would not have any trouble disposing of a few minor civilians to get to me. In fact, they probably would have enjoyed it. The clerics nowadays did. It seemed as though the old order would finally die.

Fusion cuffs, cold and hard against my skin, clamped around my wrists.

"Malachi Jones, you are hereby served and arrested for crimes against the Federated Nations, against the Science Conglomerate, against *Nexus Seven-two-one*, and against Judicial Clerical Court. You will be delivered, in stasis, to Protocol Alpha to be rendered for your crimes."

I kept my head up and eyes straight as they marched me through the long tunnel. Eyes stared. Voices whispered and murmured. Yeah, they now knew. A mass murderer stood in their midst. Worked beside them. Some had even called him friend.

My throat closed at the thought of what I was now leaving behind. The last two years on this moon had some joy to it. It might have been hard work, but it was honest work. Most of all it was freedom.

I marched in sync with them. My death awaited. No trial for me. No jury. Only a judge. And only one interview.

I was labeled a murderer. I was convicted of a crime. No matter what I had done that day, no matter what choice I made, this fate would have awaited me, nevertheless.

I was destined to death if I didn't. I was destined to Hell if I did.

# CHAPTER TWO

# DEATH IS HERE

When he had first arrived, it was a shock. A narrow band of light broke through my darkness. So bright it burned my eyes. I squinted against the pain. The narrow line quickly grew into a doorway. Three yellow cleric guards stepped into the room, followed by a man in white. Silver piping ran down his arms, torso, and legs. The interviewer.

The one thing about the Judicial Clerical Court was that no matter the crime, no matter the political turns in government, no matter the person, each story was recorded, never altered, and always on display for the populace. Too many times in the course of history were the facts changed to suit whatever nation or political movement would benefit. Then along came us, the Clerics, curators of truth and history.

The man placed a chair in the middle of the room, motioned a guard to set another in front of him, and then whispered a command.

Lights were turned up until a soft illumination glowed from above. He gestured to the chair. "Sit."

Muscles groaned and bones popped as I struggled to stand. I shuffled to the seat, completely aware of the weapons concentrated on me, and sat down.

He offered a glass of water, which I eagerly accepted and gulped down. The cool drink barely alleviated my parched throat. The interviewer pulled out his notepad and scanned the screen a moment before he tapped it. A blank screen replaced my service record.

"I'm interviewer—"

"Interviewer Sartin, D. Benjamin. With Zed Order. I know who you are. I expected none less to come hear my story."

Interviewer Sartin leaned back— his eyes wide. "You are not surprised?"

"No." I smiled, and then lifted my cup. A few taps on the bottom dislodged the last droplets of water. "White Judgement will want to know what made one of their own turn against them. But I'll have them know, I did not abandon my faith nor my Order."

"You are convicted of the deaths of one thousand, five hundred, thirty-nine people, of which included fifty top level scientists, twenty high politicians, forty-three top security advisors and officers, and fifteen prominent families."

I pressed my lips together. It always boiled down to who was the richest and most influential to be deemed as the most important. "I saved seven hundred and twenty-five people; including children, women, and families."

"Yes. Mainly low-level workers, shipping merchants, and other mid-level field officers." He tapped as he talked. His eyes never left the screen.

Anger rushed through me. It must have shown on my face because the guards had their rifles trained on me in a split second.

I tamped down that rush of injustice. "You want my story?"

"That is why I am here."

I stood, turned my chair backwards, straddled it, and draped my hands over the back. A long story required comfort. "Then I have conditions."

He looked up then. There were barely any lines in his face. Soft flesh at his cheeks, a roundness to his jaw. A youngster, playing dress up. "I cannot lobby for your release. Your execution is imminent."

"My execution will happen within the hour." I motioned at his datapad. The man wanted my story, but first he needed to know how I was delivered here to this dark and metal room. "After I tell you how I came to be here, I want you to put that on voice activation. When you do, I'll tell you my conditions and they do not pertain to any lobbying."

His bright eyes stared into mine before he nodded. "Okay. Proceed."

I related how I was found, arrested, and put into stasis. After waking up from stasis, I was immediately marched to the holding room, shoved inside, and left alone. Water and food appeared three times a week. I've had only four servings, so I estimated I have been incarcerated for a week and a half. Being a part of the White Judgement as one of their top clerics did not offer the luxury of a long wait to be executed. My sentence was handed down the day I ran. I was their embarrassment, and I was to be dealt with swiftly.

I paused and waited.

The interviewer stared back at me for long seconds before turning to the portable datapad. His hands never left the screen. His fingers flew across the board, striving to write down what I had described. He stopped, tapped one more button, and looked up at me.

"I've activated the voice recording." He set the device on the floor between us. As soon as I start to talk it will begin to record me, all of me as I sat here speaking. "What are these conditions you want?"

For hours I had struggled with the concept that I was to die, but then I had always known the day would come. Once I made peace with that idea, I had a new desire. That someone would really listen to my story. That someone would take it beyond my grave, beyond the archives, and into the world. Not to let the world know what I sacrificed for them, but to let them hear the truth of what happened that day out in the blackness of space.

I looked at the interviewer. "Only one really. I want you to really listen to me. Listen closely as I tell you what happened. Take my story and let the world know."

Interviewer Sartin frowned. "The world has access to the archives anytime they want it."

"Yes, but not everyone will know that I had a story to tell. They see me, the man who killed hundreds in a cowardly act. I want them to know that there is another side to the truth. Make sure they know."

He shrugged. "I'll do what I can." His arms crossed across his chest. "Are you ready to proceed?"

Was I? Not really. Each breath brought me closer to death. On the flip side, each breath would be truth to the world.

I inhaled deeply. "Yes. It was date 23.05.19. I was on a volunteer cargo run from Nether Outpost . . ."

# CHAPTER THREE
# THE IMPOSSIBLE MISSION

**S**trange sounds were found in space.

Malachi gazed out the porthole near the starboard airlock and thought upon that statement. Every year, every trip, that saying abounded throughout the clerics and freighters. Blackness. If he turned slightly to the right a faint glow from the nearby rogue comet could be seen. Other than that, pinpoints of blue, yellow, and at times red, dotted that inky blackness. Yet there was always a sound that echoed back to him. A ping here, a thump there.

He tapped the thick glass fused inner pane. Only a few more lonely days to his volunteer run. Then the bright lights of Alpha Prime, the largest city on Protocol Alpha and home to the Clerics, would soothe his aching eyes that only saw the darkness for so long. Artificial lighting left much to be desired.

The hollow echo of the communication console pinged down the corridor. Malachi stepped away from the bulkhead and hurried down the narrow passage. His feet barely hit the metal grating before launching himself in great gallops. He would have to dial up the gravity metrics again. That was the thing about older ships. Too many parts quickly broke down.

He splayed his arms against the hatch's frame to halt his marathon sprint. The ping dinged louder in the enclosed area of the small bridge.

With a sigh, he hit the receive button and strapped into his chair. "Cleric James! About time you replied."

"Sorry, Malachi. I had to deal with intel on Clerics Scott and Mander, plus pressing matters on Doralus Four." Cleric Donovan James grinned through the display. He ran a hand through his close-cropped hair, black peppered with a liberal amount of gray. "Mind adjusting your output? I'm not receiving you well on this end."

"Apologies, old man. I'm too close to an asteroid field. The magnetic cores are hampering my boost." Malachi leaned back and propped his feet upon the dead co-pilot console. "Want to begin? I've been looking forward to this all evening. It is evening, is it not?"

"Not here on Alpha Prime." James chuckled. "You should have set your ship's time to Prime zone instead of Nether time."

"Nether Outpost only opens for shipment from quarter past eight in the morning to quarter past noon. Had to make sure I arrived in time to load the cargo. Remind me not to volunteer for any more of these freight runs."

"That bad?"

Malachi shook his head as he reached behind him for the antique leather-bound book that lay on the narrow life support console. He caressed the soft leather as he spoke. "Lonely. I should have requested at least a skeleton crew. Or enlisted Ozero for his help. And this ship has old bones. Almost as old as you!"

James' laugh, usually hearty and deep, seemed diminished by the bad connection. "It was the only ship available. And there were no available clerics to accompany you."

"I could have made do with freight personnel."

James feigned horror. "Think of the talk. A cleric with common personnel." He smiled to soften the harsh rebuke. "So many clerics hold to that way of thinking. I'm starting to wonder if any of us who believe in humbleness and charity will be left."

"Don't start, James. Ruminating about such will only lead to envy and pride." Malachi opened to the bookmarked page. "Ready?"

"You do the honors, old boy."

Malachi guffawed at the endearment. "You are ten years my junior, old man." He cleared his voice and began, "'When your fear cometh as desolation, and your destruction cometh as a whirlwind; when distress and anguish cometh upon you—'"

"Hold it, hold it! We are still in Proverbs?"

Malachi let his shoulders slump. "James, I know you are holding readings with other clerics, but I'm two weeks behind you. The null is not the best way to communicate."

"Sorry, sorry." James waved toward the screen. "Continue. I forget that you can't open through the null while in the between."

"I dropped out of the between for this. And to recharge the amps." Malachi smiled and continued, "'Then shall they call upon me, but I will not answer they shall seek me early, but they shall not find me; For that they hated knowledge, and did not choose to fear the LORD—'"

A harsh red light flashed through his console. Malachi dropped his feet from the console. "Hold on, James."

He activated the subfield communications header. One line, three words: Urgent. Respond. Zed. Space was considered cold, an unmeasurable cold. And now his body felt just as cold.

"Malachi?"

"I have to go, James. Protocol Alpha just sent a priority Zed communique. Through the subfield."

"Subfield?" The chilling look of sheer terror crossed James' face. "Not good when they send it through the in between. Message me when you can, old friend."

The null transmission ended, and Malachi opened the subfield message. The screeching noise of subspace filtered through before the image rendered into a clear holographic image of the Clerical head office and the head of White Judgement Order. The man looked weary; shadows pulled at his eyes.

"Cleric Montage." Malachi rotated his chair to face the head cleric.

"I wish I had pleasantries to give, Cleric. But time is not a luxury." He turned and accepted a film-plast from a nearby initiate. "*Nexus Seven-Two-One* has experienced a malfunction. Exotic particles from SNR 1727-41 Nebula have infiltrated the base. The exact composition of these particles are unknown, as are their effects on the systems and personnel. We lost contact at oh-eight hundred Prime zone. You are the nearest ship within range. We need you to drop your cargo, tag it for freighter recovery, and proceed to *Nexus*. Evaluate the conditions and report for further orders."

"Chances are, Cleric, that the exotic particles will also interfere with my ship's communications, too." Malachi entered the coordinates displayed below the holographic feed as he talked. "I may have to use the subfield communicator."

"That won't work, Malachi."

He paused at the head cleric's use of his given name. "Pardon?"

"We made numerous attempts via subspace through all subfields. No response. We may be facing a recovery mission versus a rescue mission. But time is of the utmost importance. We give you full authority in all decisions to be made: Article Three, Clause Seven, Amendment Fourteen-a. Be well, Cleric. You have been awarded White Judgement status, but please, report what you find before making unilateral decisions, if you can."

The transmission ended. Malachi leaned back. From First Class, Zed Order to White Judgement First Class. This wasn't how he expected his promotion.

He unbuckled the straps from his chair. "Ship, activate homing beacons on cargo links one through four. Then disengage docking port four."

Distant clangs reverberated through the metal floor as he hurried down the short narrow passageway and into the main cargo hold. He bounded through the area with gazelle-like leaps and landed hard against the bulkhead. He peered out the porthole of the inner-airlock and through the outer-airlock. Air, which crystallized immediately in the vacuum, dispersed from the chain of cargo holds, halting its flight. As his ship pulled away, the image of the cargo growing distant by the second until it was gone from sight, Malachi activated the triple locks on the airlock door and then pass-coded the keypad.

With more gazelle style leaps, he bounded back onto the bridge and strapped in. His hands moved almost in a blur as he finished the navigation protocols and deactivated the gravity metrics. His Bible floated from the console. Malachi grabbed it and tucked it behind his back and closed his eyes.

"Ship, jump on my command. Malachi. Four-three-nine. Mark!"

A violent tug forced his head against the rest and his back against the bulky Bible. He mentally counted down the seconds, thumping his finger between each count . . . nine . . . seven . . . five . . . two . . . zero. With a sigh, the pressure eased, and Malachi opened his eyes.

Strange sounds were found in space. Strange sights were found in subspace.

He closed his eyes against the whirls of red, orange, white, and purple that were dotted with dark, ominous shapes. Better to not pay attention to the unknown and rely on the known.

Malachi willed his body to relax and mentally read *The Gospel According to Mark* from memory. He could probably make it to chapter three before he reached *Nexus-Seven-Two-One*.

# CHAPTER FOUR
# DEATH IS NEAR

*hen he arose, took the young Child and His mother, and came into the land of Israel—*

Malachi's body pressed against the straps as the ship decelerated. Eyes still closed, he smiled and spoke aloud, "Off by two verses." He opened his left eye and squinted against the riot of colors outside his viewscreen. There at the nose of the ship hung a dark shape, an oily mass of blackness, then it was gone as the ship lurched from the in between to real space.

Nausea gripped at his stomach. Malachi pressed his hands against his abdomen and took three long, deep breaths to dispel the travel sickness and the dark image from his mind. He glanced at the console. The ship was twelve thousand kilometers away, but approaching fast.

Malachi unstrapped and tapped the console. "Ship, slow to five hundred kilometers at the five thousand mark decreasing by a factor of three. Hold at one thousand kilometers and scan the station."

As the ship pinged it compliance, he stood and grimaced as his feet floated inches from the plating. "Old ships!"

Malachi half floated-half stepped to the opposite wall and turn the dial for the gravity metrics. Centimeters by centimeters, his feet slowly settled against the floor and his weight followed until it was akin to normal gravity.

He set the controls on stand-by and made his way to the main cargo hold. With quick movements, he doubled checked the airlocks and panels. Then pass-coded the medical and food supply receptacles.

The ship's mechanical voice echoed into the hold. "Life signs: two thousand two hundred seventy-three. Correction: two thousand two hundred sixty-four. Top level, floor one of *Nexus Seven-Two-One* has vented atmosphere. No life signs detected on that level. Unknown radiation levels rising. Levels one and two show five-hundred rem and rising. Level three shows one hundred rem and rising. Level four is approaching five rem."

"Ship, what radiation? Why is level four showing less rem?" Malachi started down the narrow passage to the bridge and almost fell as the ship lurched to a stop. "Ship, what has happened?"

"Failsafe systems engaged. Unknown radiation particles are detected. One thousand rem."

Malachi hurried onto the bridge and activated the co-pilot console. Read-outs from the ship's diagnostic ran across the screen. "Ship, how long will you be able to withstand the particles?"

A few moments of silence hung in dead space before it answered. "Polarization of the hull will extend maximum time to one hour. Recommend all port windows shielded."

"Acknowledged." Malachi reached above him and flipped a row of toggles. Immediately, from the back of the ship to the bridge, harsh clanking sounded. From the sides of the main viewport enforced plating covered the thick glass fused pane. Space was seen no more.

"Ship, answer my previous questions."

"The radiation is unknown. Attempting to access *Nexus* logs. Data shows severe corruption. Level four is the living quarters and has triple plating. Hypothesis: plating is slowing the radiation absorption."

Malachi settled into his chair. "We will dock at level four first. Can we raise anyone on communication?"

"Negative. Interference. On continuous ping."

He nodded. With continuous ping, the closer he approached the better chances that someone would answer. He switched off the failsafe systems. "Ship, Malachi three, two, failsafe off."

"Complied."

"How far are we?"

"Two thousand kilometers."

With quick moments he activated the holographic navigation and increased the ship's speed to one hundred klicks. It would take awhile to reach the station, but it would give him time to line up his approach to the docking port.

Long minutes stretched across the silent ship when a sudden burst of garbled signals echoed in the small confines of the bridge. Malachi ran through the communications. Only one message seemed to be less corrupted.

"This is *Nomad Transport Eleven dash Five*. Do you read me, *Nexus*?"

Static warbled through the speaker before a thin voice spoke. "*Nomad*. This is Mechanic Grade Thomas Barrett. Do you read?"

"I read, Mechanic. What is the situation?"

"Unknown. Communication with levels one and two are down. Level three has initiated lockdown. The last data burst we received was a station-wide alert about foreign particles." Static hissed through the console before the man's voice returned. "I just received word from one of our medics. The radiation has increased to fifteen rem."

Malachi muted the transmission. "Ship, status on level four."

"There is a small breach between level three and level four at junction twelve. Rem is rising. Fifteen, sixteen, approaching seventeen."

With a sigh, Malachi reached under the console unit and extracted a med kit. He keyed opened the transmission and then opened the med kit. "Mechanic, how many people on your floor?"

"Fifty souls, sir."

He pulled a hypo-injector from the kit and placed it against his arm. With a hiss, the medicine pierced his skin and flowed into his bloodstream. Hopefully, that would buy him more time against any radiation.

"Mechanic, have your people at . . . " Malachi looked at the holographic schematic. " . . . docking port eight-G. Bring nothing. All items, medicine included, will have been contaminated."

"Acknowledged." The communication fell silent.

Malachi leaned against the back of his chair and keyed open a transmission to Alpha Prime. No response. "Ship, can we send a message through subspace?"

"Negative. Too much interference."

"In-between?"

"Negative. Too much interference."

Malachi closed his eyes and offered up a quick prayer, a plea. "Let me save as many as I can, please."

# CHAPTER FIVE
# THE FIRST WAVE

The *Nomad* rattled as the locking mechanism secured the ship to docking port eight-G. Malachi stood at the door and waited until the green light lit the interior of the airlock. He entered the code and the door slide open.

Once inside— the green light bathing the walls in a murky swamp color— he removed the panel next to the outer airlock. "Ship, bypass medical containment and reroute to airlock C. Activate decom."

A ping was his reply and within a few moments a spray of atomized fluid misted around him. Malachi open the visual display.

Static met him on the visual before resolving into a grainy view of a line of people waiting at the airlock. He keyed the comm unit.

"Mechanic Barrett?"

"Here, sir. I have all on this level ready to board. No possessions, just as you said."

"Good. I'm opening the airlock." Malachi punched in his code. A rush of negative pressure pulled air from the ship into the small corridor where a long line of people waited.

A man clad in a black service uniform with a battered gray cap that barely covered his riot of red hair stood at attention. "Cleric."

"Mechanic. I will rely on you to keep order among your people. Two seconds for the decom mist to cover them. Choose someone who can assist you. Those that are injured or sick, to the right near the med units. Those who are abled, to the left."

"Yessir." Barrett turned and motioned toward the nearest man. "Private Reynolds, please assist me."

Malachi stepped forward and raised his hands, grabbing the attention of all in line. "As you enter, please listen to Mechanic Barrett's instructions. Once the last person has boarded, I will close the docking port and prepare to move up to the next floor. Time is of the essence. Please move as fast and orderly as possible."

He stepped away and back through the airlock as Barrett began herding his people aboard. Malachi hurried back to the bridge and open the viewscreens to the cargo hold. Unlike civilians who could riot and become a frenzied, panicked mob, these were professionals. Scientists, merchants, and officers. They moved quickly and precisely. The right only had two people who slid to the floor, both holding their arms. Another started assisting them before becoming frustrated when the med units would not respond to her commands.

Malachi turned from the console and started down the narrow corridor to assist her. Apparently, she was on her way to him. He met her midway.

"Cleric. I have injured men. Burns from a console. I need access to the med units, please." Her dark eyes implored him, giving no measure nor hint of being intimidated by his presence.

He searched her face for a moment. "And you are?"

"Medic Sarah Ellan. I was on furlough when this happened. By the time we could respond to the alarm, all levels were in lockdown.

When Sawyer and Mills—the two men with burns— tried to bypass the communications, the consoles exploded. We are assuming that whatever effected the station effected the consoles."

Malachi motioned for her to follow him. "*Nexus* is experiencing a wave of exotic particles. It's an unknown at the moment." He stopped at the first med unit and entered his passcode. "Use this unit. Have you run a rem gauge?"

She pulled a couple of cooling pads from the unit. "Yes. All within acceptable parameters. I will administer a hypospray for all if your stock allows it."

"I'm stocked for complement of three hundred."

"Cleric!"

Malachi gave the medic one last look. The men seemed to be in competent hands. He turned to Barrett.

"The last one is in." He moved aside as Malachi closed the outer airlock and shut down the decom. "There is something I need to show you before you move to the next level, Cleric."

As Malachi followed the mechanic into the main cargo bay, he glanced around at the fifty people huddled in small groups. "Meet me on the bridge, Barrett." Malachi motioned to the nearest man and woman. "You two, names. Position."

The man rose from the floor. "I'm Daniel Barnes, Nexus Merchant, and this is my sister, Deena. We worked the export on the station."

"Merchants? Good. Then you will understand the need and importance of rationing." Malachi pulled a small holopad from his pocket, pulled a chip from the side and inserted it into the top. "Please place your thumbs here." He indicted the sensor at the top corner of the pad.

Once their thumbprints were read, Malachi removed the chip and handed it to Barnes. "Use this chip to activate the food units. Ration it wisely. I don't know how many we will board from the next levels or how long we will be on this ship until another arrives."

"Are there no one else coming?" The woman looked at him, fear replacing worry in her expression.

"They are, yet they are still a long ways out from here. I was the closest ship." He looked from her to the man. "This chip can only be used by you." At their nods, he dismissed them with a wave and met Barrett on the bridge.

"Barrett, you needed to speak?" Malachi leaned against the co-pilot chair.

Barrett handed Malachi a datachip. "This is the security footage from levels three and two just before the lockdown."

Malachi accepted the datachip and inserted into the console. As the footage played out on the holoscreen, dread fell like lead into his soul. Frame after frame showed bodies falling at their stations. Frame after frame showed people sacrificing others to escape into shielded rooms. Frame after frame showed the horror of what was to come.

# CHAPTER SIX
# BEGINNING OF THE END

Malachi closed the hatch. Seventy-five more people from level four, floor two. Each with varying degrees of burns, injuries, and sicknesses. Medic Ellan had the people sorted according to treatment. Her competence was above reproach. She moved precisely among the patients. She would have made a good cleric had she not chosen the medical path.

He opened the panel and checked the decom levels. Only twenty percent left. And no reserves. The pounding inside his head increased. There could only be one more retrieval.

And there was only twenty-five minutes left before the hull would be compromised by the particles.

Malachi replaced the panel's cover and propped against the wall. The Judicial Academy never taught this kind of scenario. His thoughts fell back onto the time when he and Cleric James face a similar situation, with one exception. There weren't so many deaths. He forced that memory back into the recesses of his mind and turned to pick his way through the mass of people. Barrett met him halfway down the bridge corridor.

"The people are settled. The floor the majority of them were on had higher rems. Medic Ellan has them sedated, yet she doesn't believe they will make it if there isn't a transport arriving soon."

"The transports are on their way. The particles are preventing communications so I cannot receive an update nor request one." Malachi stepped past him as motioned him to follow. "There is only enough decom for one more floor. Twenty-five minutes before the particles start causing ship-wide failure on the *Nomad*."

"I see." Barrett sat at the co-pilot console. "I may be able to patch through to the *Nexus* security. That will give us a better look at their data and what floors have the most people."

Malachi ran a hand over his face and fought back a sigh. "Do it. The console in front of you has all you need." He reached into the small box beside his seat and pulled out two earpieces. "Here. Stay in communication with me. I'm disabling ship-wide communications."

He inserted the small earpiece and activated it. "Ship. Switch to internal comm. Status on Federated Nations transports?"

"Unable. Interference by unknown particles."

"Ship. What are the rems on *Nexus* levels?"

"Levels rising by factor of five. Level one, level two: no life signs. Level three: unable to determine."

Malachi activated the small holoscreen by his console. "Ship. Life support of the *Nomad* update."

"Life support failure in three hours."

Barrett paused in his work and turned to Malachi. "Reroute all power from airlocks A, B, D, and E. Then reduce power from medunits by . . . " He tapped his screen. "By thirty percent. Your ship runs on fusion coils?"

"Model Z2-LKs."

"Those are older and run more power than necessary. If we reroute at least twenty percent of its power into life support, that should give us at least a day. After that, it'll be shallow breathing and blankets."

"Ship, did you hear that?"

"Affirmative."

"Proceed with rerouting power. Reduce lighting to fifty percent."

The lights throughout the ship darkened. A shudder ran through its hull and the ventilation kicked up a notch.

"Good thinking, Barrett." Malachi maneuvered the ship to the next floor and put the docking orders in stand-by. He activated the security feed. And closed his eyes against the sight. Body after body lay on the deck. It seemed like layer after layer of people, some in piles as if trying to reach the airlock before the other and climbing over their companions. Others seem to have just dropped where they stood, either near the opening or against the wall.

Barrett hissed through his teeth and stood next to Malachi's seat. "Can you enhance the feed. Right there." He touched the screen on the furthest side of the hall.

Malachi zoomed in on the location. There in the corner, a ragged hole gaped, leading to the harsh conditions of space. As they watched another tore through the plating, ripping through the bodies and into the floor below.

"Ship. Analyze level three, floor four. Breach in the hull."

"Micro-asteroids. Possible source: asteroid field between the nebula and *Nexus Seven-Two-One*."

"Condition of level three?"

"No life signs detected on floors two to four. Interference on level three, floor one."

Malachi started to position the ship for the next docking when an impact slammed against the *Nomad*. He caught himself against the console. Barrett was flung against the far wall. Emergency klaxons sounded throughout the ship; its blare on the verge of rupturing his eardrums.

He flipped two toggles above his head and the sound died. Barrett picked himself up off the floor and floated inches from the decking.

Malachi pointed to the panel by the mechanic. "Grav metrics."

With a nod, the younger man turned to the controls and he slowly floated down until he stood on the deck. Malachi turned on the ship's schematics. Three red, pulsing dots indicated hull breaches. Port side, airlock A. Port side, cargo hold viewport. Engine three relay.

A shudder shook the ship.

"Barrett, run a diagnostic. Assess damages and take care of it."

The mechanic nodded. "I'll do it from the engineering hold." He disappeared out of the bridge.

With less power, it was now going to be even more difficult. He keyed his earpiece. "Ship, hail Medic Ellan and Merchant Barnes."

"Acknowledged." The communication pinged and the ship's hollow voice spoke. "Medic Ellan. Merchant Barnes. To the bridge. Medic Ellan. Merchant Barnes. To the bridge."

As Malachi awaited their arrival, he keyed opened communications and tried to send a message to Alpha Prime. Static. He keyed opened another channel to the station. Static.

"Cleric?"

He turned. The medic stood just inside the doorway. A worried frown creased her dark skin. The merchant looked over her shoulder, waiting.

"There were three micro-asteroid hits. Any injuries sustained?"

"Nicks and bruises only, Cleric."

"How about the people, Merchant. Are you still able to maintain order?"

"Yessir." Merchant Barnes shifted his feet. "It was a touch-and-go for a moment, but we are professionals, and these asteroids are not uncommon to us."

"Good. Have you doled out the first round of rations?"

"Yessir. Except for you and Mechanic Barrett, sir."

Malachi waved his statement off. "Think of the people first, Barnes. Barrett and I will deal with ourselves later." He stood and clapped a hand on each of their shoulders. "You two are doing a great job. Things are about to get rough, and I need to make sure you can handle what's to come. Life support is failing. We've rerouted systems to buy us time. The calmer the people are, the better our chances."

"Understood, sir." Barnes gave a nod and Malachi let him return to the hold.

He squeezed the medic's shoulder to stop her as she turned to leave. "Wait a moment, Ellan."

"Sir?"

"I need you to administer a light sedative to the people."

Deep furrows formed between her eyebrows. "Sir? That's against protocol."

Malachi stepped forward until he was looking down onto her. He spoke in as quiet as a voice as he could. "Under Article D9, section K of the Judicial Clerical Court, all medics under the supervision of a cleric must obey all orders and commands. Do you understand? I need these people calm, relaxed, and using small amounts of energy if we are to survive."

Medic Ellan swallowed hard and nodded. "I understand, Cleric. I will see to it."

He placed his hand on her arm. "Good. I am trusting you with their lives while on this ship, Ellan."

"Yessir." She tore from his grasp, face ashen, and hurried down the corridor.

Malachi stretched his neck to the side. Tendons popped and crunched as he worked the tension out of the muscles. He returned to the navigation. Only twenty minutes remaining before the hull was compromised.

It would be a miracle if the transports arrived in time. He maneuvered the ship into position for the next docking.

On the screen Nexus was in a slow spiraling spin.

# CHAPTER SEVEN

# DEATH ORDERS GIVEN

**M**alachi fought against the illusion of disorientation. There were no concepts of up and down in space. Just a big nothingness. Yet his mind saw only a spinning station and a ship that was trying to match its velocity.

He reached above him and dialed back the speed of the *Nomad*. Bit by bit, his ship realigned with the station. Distant pops echoed as it docked with the airlock and locked on.

With a few quick commands on the nav, Malachi set the ship to compensate for any change in velocity or vector, allowing it to move with the station as it performed a slow ballet toward the nebula.

The security feeds from *Nexus* faded in and out on the screen. But it didn't matter how clear the connection was. It was enough to show what was heading their way. He closed his mind against the carnage and betrayal on the screen and shut off the security connection.

Barrett slammed into the hatchway as the ship pitched sharply before the grav metrics kicked in. He rubbed his shoulder as he talked. "I have the breaches sealed. The airlocks are purged and triple-coded. The relay is damaged too badly, so I rerouted the power from it and into the others to compensate for its loss."

Malachi stood and opened a small compartment above his head. "We are going to have trouble with this next one." He pulled two pulse-fire pistols from the rack and handed one to Barrett. "Press the green button to activate the biometrics."

Barrett accepted it as color drained from his face. "How bad?"

"Security feed just cut out, but what I saw is not good. They may not try to shoot their way in, but I won't take that chance." Malachi pushed past him and strode to the airlock. Reynolds stood at attention. "At ease, Reynolds, and join the rest of the crew. You won't be needed for this one."

Confusion danced across the young man's face before he nodded once and hurried to the far side of the cargo bay. Malachi glanced over the people who populated his ship. The dim lighting cast an eerie red glow about them. Heads were down, mostly propped on knees or against the bulkhead. Some lay on the floor, sharing blankets as they huddled together. Medic Ellan moved gracefully among them. He glanced up at the top of the bay; the first threads of frost had grown.

They didn't have much time left. He approached the medic and waited until she finished administering the sedative to her patient. When she looked up at him, he pointed to the far corner where the entrance to his private quarters stood. "In my bunk are cleric robes. Use them for blankets. It's going to get a lot colder in here."

She nodded once before moving away from him. Medic Ellan knew without being told how dire their situation was—how bad it was going to get before too long.

This wasn't a new feeling. Yet he was getting tired of these situations. Impossible missions. Impossible choices. Was it the needs of the many outweigh the needs of the few? What about the one? Wasn't the one just as important as the many? Did the outcome justify the means? Was it better to justify the means instead of the outcome?

His faith was black and white. There was good and evil, wrong and right, sin and forgiveness. But life didn't believe in his faith. It always placed him in a position where his faith was tested.

Malachi took a deep breath and squared his shoulders, rejoining Barrett where he stood. "Stay right here, Barrett. I don't expect anyone to get through, but I want to take no chance." Then he walked into the airlock.

The visual display still showed an empty corridor. For now.

"Ship, what are the radiation levels for level three, floor one?"

"Unable to determine. Too much interference."

"Last known levels?"

"Last known levels at eight thousand rems."

Malachi closed his eyes and leaned his forehead against the bulkhead. "Oh, Lord, I must protect these people. Why do I have to sentence the rest to die?" But they were already dead. The old phrase 'dead man walking' crept into his mind.

He couldn't allow them to infect his people. The ship was already cycling through the automatic decom procedure. Malachi ripped the plating from the panel, reached in, and yanked a handful of wires from the circuits. Main, backup, and the backups for the backup were now disabled. Old ships. Not enough redundancy in them. What he once thought of as a curse was now a blessing.

Malachi glanced back at Barrett. The man's eyes held a horror that Malachi had only seen on the battlegrounds. With a shaky hand, the younger man reached up and removed his earpiece.

"I think it best, sir, if I don't hear what comes next." A hard swallow followed his statement. "I trust your judgement. No one can survive those levels."

"Join your people, Barrett. And take your rations. You've done well."

"If it's all the same, sir, I would like to continue monitoring the engines and life support."

"Proceed." Malachi turned back to the airlock. "Ship, how much time would be considered safe if I unshielded the airlock viewport?"

"Estimate no more than four point forty-seven minutes."

The visual display flickered. Malachi thumped its screen, and the image cleared a bit. A steady line of people started filing into the corridor. They moved fast and then even faster before breaking into a run. The run became a mad scramble toward *Nexus'* airlock.

Within seconds the reason for the panic came into view. Three clerics pushed and shoved through the throng of people. Pulse-fire pistols fired point blank into many of the people's faces and heads. The feed's gray-toned display showed the smear of gore on the bulkhead as dark blotches against a dark gray.

Malachi flinched as one of the shots tore through a woman's chest and into the neck of her shorter companion. He raised the shielding on the viewport.

*Nexus'* airlock opened and the clerics piled inside. Two of Zed order and one of Delta order. Malachi locked eyes on the Zed order cleric, the one who killed the woman and her companion. He was of the third grade. The other was an initiate. But she should have known better than to betray her faith. The Delta order was older. Yet his face was just as hardened as the other man's.

The Zed order keyed the communication console. "Cleric, I'm Davie Horndale, Second grade, Yellow Justice class, Zed order. This is Bonnie O'Dell, Initiate grade, Blue Justice class, Zed order. John DeVine, First grade, White Curator class, Delta order. We request permission to come aboard!"

Malachi peered past them at the bodies that laid in the corridor. Some still moved. Their hearts may still have been beating, but they were already dead.

He hit the comm. "Clerics, you have absorbed too many rems and will infect those on board. Permission denied."

"Cleric!" Horndale battered his fist against the viewport. "You cannot abandon others of your order! I demand that you let us on board!"

His companions tightened their grips on their weapons.

He had never known hate before. Dislike and disgust, yes. But to feel pure hatred for another. That was foreign to him. Yet seeing those three standing before him, betrayers to the faith and to the order . . . betrayers to their Lord.

Malachi posed his hand over the emergency release. "Clerics. I am Malachi Jones, Cleric First grade, White Judgement First class, Zed order."

Their faces paled.

He could see a faint reflection of his own face as he pronounced their judgement—dark blue eyes glaring in anger. Never had he seen his eyes so cold and ruthless. "I sentence you to death for your crimes against the members of *Nexus-Seven-Two-One*, Level three, Floor one. Judgement is served. Punishment forwent. Execution . . . " Malachi keyed in the dock release commands. " . . . forthwith."

The locks released. Atmosphere was ripped into the void as the *Nomad* shot away from the airlock. The dead and the dying in the corridor careened against the bulkheads and walls. The three sentenced clerics joined them, not having the mercy, time, or breath to scream. What remained became debris that tumbled, twirled, and spiraled through space . . . a macabre parody of a dance.

Malachi shut down the display. Then he returned to the bridge without a backward glance.

The console was pinging. A signal from *Nexus* had succeeded in coming through.

"*Nexus Seven-Two-One.* Emergency Protocol. This is *Nexus Seven-Two-One*, emergency protocol has been initiated . . . "

"This is the *Nomad*. Do you read?"

"*Nomad. Nexus Seven-Two-One.* We are on level three, floor two. Floor one has vented. We have minimum life support. And three hundred souls."

He glanced at the readings on his nav display. Ten thousand rems. And rising.

"I'm sorry." Malachi whispered the words. "You are already dead."

Weariness and sadness crept into his heart as he closed communications with *Nexus*. Their cries and pleading ended abruptly. Barrett entered the bridge.

"We cannot save them, sir."

"I know."

Barrett handed him a film-plast. "I downloaded this from long-distance radar before diverting power. I hope you don't mind that I contacted them."

Even though a small smile inched across his face, Malachi's heart felt like lead. "How many on the emergency transport?"

"About six hundred, sir. They were able to evacuate on the Class-Four Transport."

Which could hold an accompaniment of nine hundred, easily. Malachi entered the communication codes into his console. The signal was strong. "Barrett, contact them. We will dock with them and tow them out of the region. What is their exposure?"

"Nil. They had less than us."

"Good. We can use their supplies to help those in the cargo bay." Malachi stood and placed his hand on Barrett's shoulder, giving it a hard squeeze. "You would have made a great Cleric, Barrett. You performed amazingly well."

"Thank you, sir. I'll use the comm in the cargo bay." Barrett hurried away.

Malachi sat back down. "Ship, can we open communications to Protocol Alpha?"

Two pings later the ship responded. "Negative. Interference."

"What were the two pings?"

"Intercepted signal. Corrupted message. Cannot read."

Malachi sighed and leaned back in his chair. His Bible laid to the side of the console. He picked it up and brought it to his chest. "Ship, notify me when we have reached minimum safe distance to open shielding."

He closed his eyes and waited. Waited until he could see space. Waited until he could send Protocol Alpha a message. Waited until he could dock with the transport.

And he would be waiting until his own death orders were given.

# CHAPTER EIGHT
# ETERNAL LIFE AWAITS

I let my hands drop to my knees and waited on Sartin to absorb my story. His face mirrored the same horror I saw on Barrett's face all those years ago.

My mind replayed the days and months afterwards. Another ship had been found on the other side of the asteroid field. Damaged, but they had made an amazing discovery concerning the composition of the asteroids. That discovery provided the Federated Nations the ability to conduct a recovery mission on all the lost souls of *Nexus*.

After that, my punishment for allowing them to die—despite the medical field professionals stating that they were beyond help—was issued. For months, the Judicial Clerical Court held them at bay, protecting me. Shunting me off to the distant planets and colonies for my own safety . . . until Cleric James, my one ally, died. That was when my death orders were given.

Then I ran.

"You were faced with an impossible choice." Sartin slumped in his chair. "Why did you dock in the first place?"

"It was my intention to inform them that they could not come aboard, or they would infect their fellow workers. And to give them assurance that another ship would come, whether it was an empty promise or not, they deserved a bit of hope." Sorrow poured from his eyes. "Yet when I saw the clerics . . . what they did."

"You have every right to be heard by the Court. To lobby for your life."

"No." I shook my head. He was still young. New to the faith and to the order. "I lost that right the moment I ran. When I left the order, when I abandoned my brethren, I forfeited any chance to lobby for my life. That is my sin and I have to live with the consequences. Well, at least live with it for the next few moments."

"Your sin?" Sartin shook his head. He glanced at the datapad that still recorded the conversation. "You were afraid. Surely that is understandable."

"Cleric Sartin, you will soon learn that we cannot allow fear to govern our thoughts and actions. Our faith is placed in the Lord. I should have allowed Him to guide me. I should have stayed and let the truth be shown. Yet I didn't. I let fear dictate me. I placed fear of death, fear of my own life being taken away, fear of people's judgement over my trust in the Lord." I smiled. The doors opened and a group of Zed order clerics stepped inside. "What I did that day, saved many lives. What I allowed myself to do, it was done out of hate, not justice. My heart was wrong. To the universe, I am being executed for allowing hundreds of people to die on that station, even though they were beyond help. Yet to me, I am being justly punished for killing three clerics in cold blood because there was hate in my heart."

"But no one knows your heart, Cleric Jones." Sartin stood, allowing the datapad to continue recording.

"I do. The Lord Jesus does." I rose from my chair and turned around, hands at my back. Two of the clerics stepped forward and clamped the fusion cuffs around my wrists, yet they waited patiently as I talked to Sartin. "And now others will, too. What those three clerics did was wrong, was evil. But we are to bring our own to Protocol Alpha for judgement. Clerics are exempt from summary judgement, Sartin."

"But you weren't on that moon, Cleric Jones."

"I am no longer a cleric. I am just Malachi Jones." I nodded toward the datapad. "I release you from the conditions I set forth."

Sartin picked up the datapad and held it, the red light still flashing as it recorded an audio and visual record. "The truth has to be told."

"And it has been." I looked at the cleric next to me. "Let's go."

"Wait!" Sartin started to step toward me but paused when the other clerics stepped forward. "I have more questions, Malachi. Are you in such a hurry to die?"

I turned from him and started walking to the door. Before I crossed the threshold, my elbows held by the two clerics on either side of me, I peered over my shoulder at Sartin. "I'm not heading to death, Benjamin. I am heading to my eternal life. Execution awaits me in this world, but Heaven awaits me in the next."

I left him there. The datapad still flashed red.

The *thump-thump* of our boots echoed in the stark white halls. Execution would be swift. A quick injection. A drowsy feeling. Then I would awake in a world where no more hate, evil, death, or sadness existed.

The cleric next to me whispered. "I believe you, Cleric Jones. And many of us, including Cleric Ozero, lobbied for your life."

I glanced at him. "I know, Cleric Samuels."

"You know me?"

"Yes, I do." I paused outside the medical room where the automated procedure awaited. "Remember your faith, Cleric. Always offer a second chance. Don't let evil pervert our order."

With that I stepped inside and onto the platform. The door closed, shutting off the cleric's expression of grief, and I leaned against the upright bed. Metal bands closed over my chest, hips, legs, and feet. A slight hiss was the only indication that the drug had been administered into my spine.

Warmth spread quickly. My eyelids grew heavy. The cool, wetness of a tear tracked down my cheek which started growing numb. One thought escaped as darkness settled in . . . they may think I was crying because I was dying. But I wasn't. I was crying because I would soon be living.

*After a dangerous heist goes south, Bhirus finds sanctuary with his fellow Upper Thieves in one of their clandestine safeships. Once aboard, he begins to suspect that the ship's crew may not be what they seem, and he finds himself confined to a safeship that may be anything but safe.*

# SAFESHIP

## P.S. PATTON

# CHAPTER 1
# THE TIGHTNESS

*If a thief is caught breaking in at night and is struck a fatal blow,*
*the defender is not guilty of bloodshed.*

Exodus 22:2 (NIV)

His lungs always gave out before his legs did. Ever since Bhirus was a kid he'd suffered from the tightness in his lungs. It only really became a problem when he ran for too long. This wasn't the first time he had to push through his handicap for the sake of the job, but this was certainly the longest chase he'd ever endured. His eyes scanned the jilting horizon for the telltale signs of a safeship, hoping to find one before his indignant bronchioles seized up completely.

The baying of netherhounds somewhere behind him spurred him onward through Reynolds Interstellar Spaceport. He didn't even feel the skin rip away from his left shoulder as he barreled down a packed corridor, veering too close to the rusted and twisted wire fencing. He emerged at the far end of the corridor knowing full well that this next terminal would be his last chance. The terminal was too large and too open. The nearest exit might as well have been a distant planet, and he wouldn't get there alive without some albuterol to dilate his constricting airway.

He spotted a posse of spaceport security dead ahead of him. They had seen him as well. Hands dropped in unison, releasing loose grips on black radios and unholstering fully-charged hotshots with ice-dancer synchrony.

Then he saw it, scrawled in the merciful hue of mercenary blue across the hull of a Saber-class freighter: the secret runes known only to Upper Thieves. It was a safeship. Bhirus would be happy to surrender a quarter of his score of the job at that point—he would have given them half if they demanded it, but he knew they wouldn't do that. Upper Thieves lived and died by the code.

To his right, he caught a flash of yellow. He hoped it wasn't what he thought it was. He turned and saw the thing he feared. Three clerics—Gamma patrols—were bearing down on him quickly. He was sure he could beat them to the ramp, but he'd have to book it if they were going to lift the ramp and take off before the clerics caught up. Somewhere behind him, the baying of the netherhounds grew closer.

The captain stood vigilant at the bottom of the ramp, ready to beat feet if the right opportunity came along. Bhirus was close, but the world was growing increasingly unstable around him, swirling and spinning, blinking and bobbing. Was he even running toward the ship, or was it getting further from him? With the safeship just out of grasp, a ruthless desperation snuck in a solid punch to the gut, and he was suddenly sure that he'd never make it. If the netherhounds didn't catch him and crush his windpipe with their reaping jaws, then the tightness would—and the tightness wasn't called off so easily.

The captain of the safeship turned in Bhirus' direction and met his gaze. Bhirus's thoughts landed on his own uniform. He was disguised as a Marash House guard, as the job had called for. Any good safeship captain should be able to recognize the situation and see past the disguise, but it still made him nervous. He'd never had to don a disguise for a job before, and he'd certainly never botched a job so badly that his life depended on a safeship.

To his relief, the captain nodded, and an unspoken agreement had been made, simple as that. She disappeared up the ramp and a moment later the engines roared to life, blending into the ubiquitous hum of the spaceport terminal. The netherhounds behind him grew louder and the ship before him grew darker. His legs threatened to fold up and he was no longer breathing at all. He forced his eyes open and saw the ramp just a few steps ahead of him. His eyelids forced themselves shut again as he took the final few steps in darkness.

# CHAPTER 2

# TEA WITH LAVENDER

*Upon the wicked he shall rain snares, fire and brimstone, and an*
*horrible tempest: this shall be the portion of their cup.*

Psalms 11:6 (KJV)

He heard the blessed metal clanging beneath his feet, and he fell forward, collapsed onto the ramp and rapidly sucked at whatever precious air his constricted airway could manage. There was a mechanical whirring and a sudden jolt followed by a steady rising sensation as the ramp retracted and pulled him up out of Reynolds Interstellar Spaceport and into the arms of safety. A pair of hands jabbed themselves under his arms and clumsily dragged his prone body to the center of the hull. A deep female voice called out.

"Wake up."

He was half awake. Bhirus managed to roll to his left side, ignoring the pain in his shoulder where he'd been snagged by the wire fencing, and yanked on the strap to release his pack. He unzipped one of the smaller pockets with a numb right hand. He seemed to have lost all command of his arm, and only when he looked directly at it could he do anything useful with it. His hands were already becoming cyanotic.

He pulled his puff-box out of his pocket, brought it to his lips, and breathed in the aerosolized drug with as deep a breath as he could manage. His heart rate increase almost instantly. The stars around him intensified, their lights effectively blinded him, and the dark, dancing figure above him confused him. He puffed again and wondered at the waves of pulsing light and the jumble of senseless shapes which moved around him.

"Wake up!"

The woman's voice was followed by a hard *thwap* across his jaw. It addled his brain a bit, but it hardly concerned him. He held up a hand and nodded to signal that he understood the command. All around him, senseless shapes began to settle into a more comprehensible setting. He was in the cargo hold of the safeship surrounded by crates, boxes, empty shelves, stacks of pallets, a pallet-pusher secured against the wall, a work bench scattered with various tools, a tool chest, and a set of lockers. He was going to be okay.

"What's your name?" she asked.

"Bhirus," he spat out between rapid and shallow breaths. "Bhirus Andrus."

"Well let's get you upright, Bhirus Andrus."

The woman shoved her arm beneath his back and lifted. He went with it and raised himself up, then he rested his arms on his knees in a tripod position. The tightness was dissipating, and he was now fully aware of his surroundings. The woman leaning over him now was not the captain he had seen at the foot of the ramp. This second woman had a hard face and a sturdy frame.

"What was your take?" She asked with a stupid smirk.

"Didn't count. Just took. What I could. In the pack."

"It'd better be worth blowing our cover at Reynolds," she grumbled, getting to her feet. "Follow me."

He slowly raised himself up and followed the large woman through a door, through the airlock and into the small galley. A square table and four chairs sat in the center, all bolted to the steel galley floor. She motioned vaguely toward the table.

"Siddown."

He obeyed. He slung his pack onto the back of a chair and sat. As he rested against the cold and unmoving steel chair, his own body pulsed against it, his heart thumped furiously in his chest. Bhirus watched the mean-eyed woman opening cabinets, pulling things out and clinking glasses around. The choked tings of rattling silverware caused him to wince.

His mind wandered back to the miserable job. His small band of upper thieves was dead. He hadn't quite had the opportunity to process that fact yet. He knew they were dead, but he was very aware that he hadn't really allowed himself to feel the impact of it yet.

Was he in denial? No. This wasn't the first time a brother or sister had been killed in action. He'd push himself on through to safety and make it back to the den, and then he'd feel it. Tomorrow. For a while after that. Forever, to some extent. Once the shock wore off, the grief would sink its teeth into his soul. He knew it wouldn't do him any good to think about it now, not until this was over. He forced himself to snap out of it.

"What's your name?" Bhirus asked.

She turned and shot him a look of dumb amusement, then turned back to resume her clinky work. "Lavender."

"Lavender?" Bhirus asked.

The woman slapped a utensil onto the counter and paused her work. "That's what I said, innit?"

"Didn't mean anything by it."

Lavender let out a slow and controlled breath. She clearly never had any patience to run out of. She turned and placed a tray on the steel table with a clang. Atop the tray was a quick-boil pitcher, three saucers, three teacups already filled with water, and tea bags steeping. Bhirus hated tea, but he thought the hot steam might help loosen up the tightness in his lungs. He reached out for the nearest cup, then paused and reached for a second cup instead. The cup he chose was neither the closest nor the furthest from him.

"Thank you," he sighed.

Lavender stared at him with an irritating and stupid smirk. "Did you really just do that?"

Of course he just did that. He was not an idiot. If she took offense that easily, she was in the wrong business. He held the cup to his lips, let the tea lap up against his pursed lips, but he didn't dare let the vile stuff in. Instead, he simply breathed in the hot flavored vapors.

Lavender watched him intently. Why was she staring at him with such a cautious anticipation? He'd taken the middle teacup more out of habit than out of any real suspicion, but after her reaction he was starting to wonder.

No. He was being paranoid. If she'd poisoned him, she wouldn't be dumb enough to stare like that. It was such an obvious giveaway. Still, something was not sitting right in his gut. Could she actually be that dumb? If she really was an upper thief, she couldn't be dumb. That was just it, though—was she really an upper thief? Of course she was. There was no way of infiltrating the upper thieves and commandeering a safeship. Was there? He was starting to have his doubts.

No. There was no way they could have procured this ship, those uniforms, and those patches. If she was somehow an imposter, she had nailed every detail of the charade. He doubted it could be possible—still he knew better than to ignore his gut. He placed his teacup down on the saucer and let out an over-the-top *ahhhhh* in an attempt to sell his satisfaction. It worked. Lavender's anticipation tightened into a crooked half smile.

"So what was the job?" she asked.

"Marash House."

"Big target," she huffed. "How'd you manage to pull that off?"

"We didn't," Bhirus sneered. "I wouldn't be sitting here in the pleasure of your company if we did."

Lavender sneered back at him. Her expression threatened that he'd better be joking.

# CHAPTER 3
# ANYTHING BUT SAFE

*For when they shall say, Peace and safety; then sudden destruction cometh upon them, as travail upon a woman with child; and they shall not escape.*

1 Thessalonians 5:3 (KJV)

The cockpit doors opened, and the captain entered the galley. Up close, she looked even prettier than he'd first realized, but real rough around the edges.

"Marash House, huh? So, we've got ourselves a real hero of the people."

Bhirus shrugged and showed a skeptical smile.

The captain continued. "Stickin' it to ol' Marash, eh? I like that. Of all the self-righteous Science Conglomerate Elites, Marash is the biggest crook of them all if you ask me. He was overdue. Had it comin'. Been waitin' a long time for an honest thief to settle the score with ol' Marash."

"There is no such thing as an honest thief," Bhirus corrected her.

The captain returned a wry smile.

"Now don't go crushin' my dreams like that, brother. I'd like to think that one day I'll find myself an honest thief to settle down with. Someplace nice. Take only the sweetest jobs, you know? One or two jobs a year, max." Her eyes sent subconscious signals that he couldn't quite decode, though he suspected this was her way of flirting. He leaned forward and tried his best to appear impervious to the captain's intentions. He wasn't about to break the code, and this raised his suspicions even more.

"If it's the western shore you seek," Bhirus said, "best not linger in the east."

The captain cocked her head and squinted her eyes, apparently unsure what to make of her new passenger. Lavender stared at the captain with wide eyes and parted lips, like a child waiting for her mother to turn the page and tell her what happens next.

"It means if you want an honest man, you're wasting your time picking up on thieves," said Bhirus.

"Yeah, I got it," the captain smiled. "What fellowship hath the wolf with the lamb and all that."

Bhirus had no idea what that meant, and made it known with a blank expression.

"It's from Ecclesiastes," the captain said.

Bhirus shook his head slowly. He had no idea what this lady was talking about.

"From the Bible, man! Come one! Someone's been skipping church on Sunday."

Another red flag. The Upper Thieves had no religious or political affiliations that could act as a conflict of interest. It's possible she was using the Bible as a pop-culture reference, but his gut told him otherwise.

"Anyways." The captain held out a firm hand to Bhirus. "I'm Vinia."

"Bhirus."

"Nice to have you aboard," she said, rising to her feet.

"I'd be dead if your ship wasn't there. I want to thank you properly for your service. Standard fee?"

"We're glad to be of service. I'm sure you're exhausted after getting chased through Reynolds. Big place. Nowhere to hide."

Again, the overly expectant look. Had they drugged the tea? There was only one way to find out.

"I am," Bhirus said, then forced the most convincing yawn he could muster. "I shouldn't be so sleepy, but I am. I can hardly keep my eyes open to be honest."

"Then rest. Once you finish your tea, Lav will show you to the guest berth. We can settle up later once you're rested."

He'd never had to use a safeship before, but it still seemed to him that something was very wrong with this situation. She hadn't even asked his destination. This was not good. Where were they taking him? He thought he'd stand a good chance against these two, but there were likely others on board. For now, he thought it best to go with it until he could figure out what game they were at.

Bhirus smiled back at Captain Vinia and held up his teacup as if to offer a toast. Vinia's gaze lingered on him until she exited the galley leaving Bhirus alone with Lavender once again. He held his teacup to his lips and breathed in the steam into his tight lungs. Lavender's eyes were fixed firmly on the cup once again. The captain had managed to act normal enough, but red flags were flying with this one.

He avoided eye contact and acted as if everything was normal, careful not to let any tea cross the barrier of his tightly pressed lips. This wasn't going to work if she continued to monitor him so closely.

If the tea really was poisoned, what then? Would they simply take his money and run? Would they dump him on some rural continent with no money and no transportation? Would the poison kill him? Would his cold body be jettisoned out into the eternal darkness of the null or the in-between?

An idea popped into his head. He set his teacup down onto its saucer and then grabbed his pack from behind him. He reached in and removed a small stack of bills, then he tossed them over to Lavender.

"I just hope we didn't get duped by a decoy again," Bhirus acted the part of an anxious fool, angry with himself for his own failure. "They've been sending out decoy cars lately, filled up with bad bills. They look exactly like the real thing."

Lavender inspected the bills in her hand, flipped the stack over, and then back again.

"Looks real to me," she raised an eyebrow.

"Of course they do. That's the point. Bankers are the only ones who can tell the difference between the real deal and the decoys."

Bhirus shrugged. Lavender sighed with annoyance and then peeled the paper binding away. She slid one bill off the top of the stack and held it up in front of the overhead light, staring up at the bill, looking through it for signs of a counterfeit.

That was exactly what Bhirus was hoping for. He quickly and silently moved his teacup below the table and let it pour onto the steel galley floor. By the time she was done inspecting the bill, the teacup was back on the saucer.

"It's legit," Lavender said. "We'll count it all in the morning and figure out what you owe us for saving your life. For now, just finish your tea so you can get some sleep."

He noted that both women had now been sure to remind him that he was to finish his tea. At least Captain Vinia was subtle about it. Lavender was about as subtle as a broken nose. He might not have noticed anything suspicious about the captain's behavior had he not already been so on edge due to Lavender's clumsy approach.

What did they want from him? Easy. They wanted money. It always came down to money. They wanted to poison him, then rob him. They wanted more than the standard quarter of the take. They wanted all of it. These were no upper thieves. Praying on uppers broke every code there was. They weren't even mids or lowers. These were bottom feeders—no code, no honor, no shame. The skulking scum of the universe.

Bhirus figured the best thing to do now was to get to his room where he was expected to fall asleep. Once alone and without distraction, maybe he'd be able to think this through and come up with a plan. One thing was for sure, though—this safeship was anything but safe. With nowhere to run and nothing to do but ride it out, he'd have to step carefully if he hoped to get off this ship alive.

## CHAPTER 4
# One Step Ahead

*Let the wicked fall into their own nets, while I pass by in safety.*

Psalm 141:10 (NIV)

**B**hirus held the empty teacup to his lips and feigned a final gulp, then followed it with a satisfied *ahhhhh*. He wiped his lips with his uniform sleeve and thanked Lavender for the tea. The mean-eyed woman rose to her feet and watched Bhirus expectantly. She really didn't have a single subtle cell in her large body, that one. He wondered why Captain Vinia bothered keeping her around.

As he rose to his feet, he thought of the tea he hadn't drunk. Lavender would be expecting him to . . . what? Die? Sleep? Stumble? Should he have passed out by now? He tried to read her reaction, but she didn't seem to react at all. She simply watched him as he stood. If they were poisoning him, and if they knew that he knew, the gig would be up. He decided to do his best impersonation of a drunken man. If she looked surprised, then perhaps the tea wasn't poisoned after all. If she acted as if that's what she'd expected to happen, he'd know it was poison for sure.

They exited the galley down a corridor and Lavender showed not the least bit of concern over his sloppy gait. She simply showed him to the guest berth which consisted of a set of two bunks, one atop the other, and nothing else. It wasn't difficult to act drugged, in fact it was hardly acting at all. He was exhausted, he simply exaggerated his heavy eyes and lethargic movements. Bhirus flopped down on the bottom bunk and played dead, open-mouthed and slack-jawed. He memorized the expression and the position of his limbs in case she returned.

The door closed. His eye opened. Just enough. She was gone. He lay still. And heard voices. He crept to his feet and pressed up against the door. He forced his heart to slow down. To slow way, way, way, down. Then Bhirus focused his attention on the voices coming through the wall. They were coming from the galley, and he was confident that if he needed to, he could quickly and quietly return to the position that Lavender had left him in. His right hand moved instinctively to three o'clock, securing itself around the grip of his hotshot. It was probably just the wall between them, but it sounded to him as if both women were speaking with mouths full.

"Marash House confirmed he's not one of ours. He's an Upper," Lavender said.

*Not one of ours? Who were they exactly?*

"Copy that," said Vinia. "I'm setting course for Protocol Alpha. We'll deliver the suspect and fuel up at Alpha Prime, then we'll head back to Marash House."

*Alpha Prime?* Bhirus' heart nearly stopped. *The Judicial Clerical Court was on Alpha Prime.*

Then it sank in. All the way in. These were Marash House Guards, disguised as Upper Thieves. Marash must have planted a mole on the job. It was the only explanation. That's why Marash was one step ahead of them at every turn. He'd known the whole time. That's why the vault room wouldn't open. That's why everything went south in such a hurry. That's why three of the bravest Upper Thieves he'd ever known were now dead. Marash had even managed to plant a counterfeit safeship at the spaceport to tie up any loose ends who managed to escape.

The tightness had never fully left him, and now it fought back hard. His face burned and the pressure was rapidly building in the increasingly claustrophobic berth. His instinct told him to start shooting—to kill them now, but he restrained himself. If he blew his cover, he'd have to face multiple combatants at once. He'd have a much better chance if he waited until Lavender returned and gave her a swift and silent grip-whip to the head. Then he might be able to sneak out of his berth and investigate further. If the Captain was the only other crew member, he'd be golden. He imagined flying himself to safety and returning the stolen vessel to the Upper Den. He would be a hero if he got out of this alive.

"So what's the verdict? Cage 'im or kill 'im?"

"Cage him. We'll deliver him to Alpha Prime for a tribunal."

"Seriously?"

"Seriously."

"Marash has all the intel we needs on the Uppers. There's no one left for him to rat on. What possible reason could we have for keeping this scumbag alive?"

"I don't know, Lav. Probably just want to make an example of him with a harsh sentence. What's the problem?"

"No problem, Vin. I just want to kill him."

"Doesn't matter what you want, Lav."

"Obviously. All right, cage 'im it is."

Behind Bhirus there was an angry whirring, then an ominous slamming noise. He turned to see a rack of metal bars shooting up out of the frame of each bunk and up toward the ceiling. This wasn't a berth; it was a brig. He was meant to be drugged and detained behind those bars. As the bars locked into place, he noticed that his pack was still on the bunk. He hit the floor and reached in as far as he could, but it wasn't far enough. Bhirus shoved his shoulder in between the bars, but the pack was just out of reach. He retracted his arm and grabbed his hotshot, hoping to use the grip to snag the strap, but before he had a chance, he heard footsteps coming down the hall toward him. They were close.

Bhirus took a deep breath. This was it. He had the advantage. Marash had managed to beat the Upper Thieves at their own game because he'd stayed one step ahead of them. Now the tables had turned, and it was Bhirus who was one step ahead of his captors. He silently positioned himself just inside the door frame, raised his hotshot over his head, and prepared to fight for his life.

# CHAPTER 5
# LONGSHOT

*The evil deeds of the wicked ensnare them; the cords of their sins hold them fast.*

Proverbs 5:22 (NIV)

The door opened. It was Vinia. She stepped inside the tiny room and immediately realized Bhirus wasn't in the bunk-brig where she'd expected to find him, and though he could see the instantaneous reaction in her eyes, her body took a moment to correct course. It was enough. Her foot carried her forward through the door allowing Bhirus to slam the grip of his hotshot down on the side of her head. Just before the impact, the captain spun in an attempt to raise her weapon and fire. Her eyes met his, and he saw fear. She was too late, and she knew it. He clobbered her, and she went down hard.

"Let's see if your God can save you now, Captain," he muttered.

He paused for a moment to listen for any sign of Lavender, but a long moment of silence seemed to indicate that she had heard nothing.

Bhirus dragged the captain's body the rest of the way into the room. She was out cold. He had to lift her legs straight up in order to get the door closed. He confiscated her hotshot and removed her radio, clipping it onto his own belt. It fit perfectly onto his Marash

House guard uniform belt. Of course it did. It was a Marash guard radio confiscated from a Marash guard. It occurred to him that every soul on board was dressed as the enemy, and the thought amused him.

He peeked out into the corridor, found it to be quiet, and then closed himself in the room once again. He switched the radio to a familiar frequency. There was a good chance Lavender would hear his radio traffic and come running, so he'd have to be quick. He keyed the radio and transmitted in the Upper Thieve's Cant so that only fellow Uppers could decipher the message.

"Calling any upper thieves in the vicinity of my transmission location. We have a Code-44. Repeat, we have a Code-44. Marash House guards are in control of one of our safeships—a Saber class Freighter with Upper Cant markings across the hull in blue. I'm an Upper Thief detained on board. Repeat, Marash House guards are in control of one of our safeships . . . "

The door flew open and slammed hard against Vinia's lifeless legs. Lavender did her best to shove through, but the captain's unconscious body prevented the door from opening wide enough. Bhirus was quick to react. He slammed his body into the door which crushed Lavender's wrist against the door frame. The woman roared, dropped her hotshot, and continued howling as she retreated out into the corridor. Bhirus tried to follow but was slowed by Captain Doorstop.

By the time he finally stumbled into the corridor and made his way to the galley, Lavender was marching toward him from the cockpit raising a newly acquired longshot. He was caught off his guard. She didn't hesitate. The weapon blasted and an explosion of sizzling sparks enveloped him. He was forced backward off his feet and his head slammed hard against the galley table, knocking him nearly unconscious.

Things went black for a second, and he felt confused, but it wasn't the first time he'd been knocked out. He was vaguely aware that he was in real trouble, and it only took a second before he knew what to do. He still had a weapon of his own. He could still fight back. He tried to raise his right hand to fire his hotshot, but his arm didn't seem to be on the same page. In fact, he couldn't feel his right arm at all. His eyes shot downward, and he was surprised to see flames dancing along the edges of his Marash guard uniform—edges that shouldn't be there—just below his right shoulder. A few feet away, his right arm rocked back and forth on the galley floor. His right hand still gripped the hotshot firmly.

A surreal slur of events followed. The tightness took hold of him, and his breathing became labored. The pain in his shoulder came on suddenly and ruthlessly, sending his mind into chaos and his body into a spasm. The ground approached quickly as he fell sideways against the steel galley floor. He felt a sick, wet splat against his cheek, and he breathed in the thick, pungent odor of tea. He hated tea.

There was a distant awareness that he had been shot, and that he needed to escape. The tightness gripped his lungs firmly and he struggled to take in air. The vibrations of Lavender's feet pounded against the steel floorboards. He rolled over. She loomed above him. She raised her boot and stomped down on his chest.

In that moment, with no course of action left to take, the only thing Bhirus could think was, "So that's why Vinia keeps her around."

Lavender dug her heel deeper into his ribs, lifted her longshot, and aimed down at him. Bhirus choked out a scream. Lavender smiled an awful smile.

# CHAPTER 6
# THE RESCUE

*How futile it is to spread the net*
*where any bird can see it!*
*But they lie in wait for their own blood;*
*they ambush their own lives.*
*Such is the fate of all who are greedy,*
*whose unjust gain takes the lives of its possessors.*

Proverbs 1:17-19 (NIV)

The ship jolted. He knew that feeling. Their ship was being force-docked by a larger ship. Upper thieves? Oh, please let it be Upper Thieves. Who else could it be? They must have heard his transmission. If there had been a band of Uppers near enough to hear his radio traffic, they would have dropped everything to come and recover the ship, and to rescue their fellow Upper. It was a matter of honor. It was their duty. It was the code.

With this new turn of events, Bhirus' mind became a little sharper. Lavender had been thrown backward off her feet by the jolt of the dock. Bhirus watched it happen as if time had congealed and was slowly oozing out from the throbbing hole in his shoulder. Even with Lavender's giant foot off his chest, the tightness had a real good hold on him now. His puff-box was in his pack, back in the bunk-brig. As his lungs starved for oxygen, his mind clung precariously at the edge of sanity. He recognized that he had to act quickly or forfeit his life. His face bounced a little when Lavender hit the floor. He rolled quickly to his right and scrambled with his left hand to grab his hotshot, prying the weapon from his own dead hand. He surprised himself at how smoothly the action was executed. He snapped his left arm back in the direction of the woman, his eyes locked in on her beyond the hotshot's sites, and he squeezed the trigger. Her chest exploded and sparks shot out from behind her in every direction.

He tried to breathe a sigh of relief, but the tightness gripped his lungs too hard even for that. He collapsed to the ground and focused on slowing his breathing. Relief was here. He'd been rescued. Now all he had to do was get his breathing under control and he'd be all right.

Somewhere behind him, he heard the familiar clangs of a boarding ramp being guided into place, followed by the horrible squeal of the freighter's ramp being forced open. Finally, the sound subsided. They'd successfully forced their way in.

Friendly Upper Thief uniforms filled the galley, and a chorus of yells broke out all at once. Upper's boots stamped past his face. He could feel someone standing over him, but he didn't bother to look up. Then a boot stamped down hard on his back. He could barely breathe before, and now the pressure on his chest was truly suffocating him.

"Drop it! Drop it now!"

Bhirus didn't question. He followed orders and dropped the hotshot. He couldn't figure out why they were . . . and then his heart fell to his gut. His uniform. He was still dressed as a Marash house guard. He replayed his transmission in his mind.

" . . . Marash House guards are in control of one of our safe ships . . . I'm an Upper Thief detained on board . . . "

From his transmission, they were aware that there was an Upper Thief prisoner held captive aboard, but here he was, dressed as a Marash House guard. He was dressed as the enemy, and this other band of Upper Thieves had no way of knowing that the uniform was simply a disguise. Everyone on board this ship had been in disguise. The thought wasn't so amusing to him now.

"I . . . I'm . . . Upper . . . Thief . . . "

"Shut up!"

The Upper Thief's boot stabbed into the back of his ribs with such force that he was certain he would die from it. He couldn't even get a single word out and his breaths were failing him completely. The world began to grow darker. He looked around the room, looking for a familiar face, one that might recognize him . . . but no. This band was unknown to him. They had simply responded to the distress call of a fellow Upper Thief.

A new figure entered the room. Bhirus's vision was spotty, but it was still obvious that the newcomer's gait garnered a natural authority. Without even seeing his patches, Bhirus knew him to be the band's Master. As he entered the galley, another Upper entered the galley from the corridor, carrying an unconscious Vinia in his arms.

"She was in the brig. She's alive, but we need to get her to the infirmary."

"Aye, bring her on board," ordered the Master.

"No . . . " Bhirus could barely get the word out. Every last bit of oxygen was expelled from his lungs with that single word. Then the boot came down hard once again, pinning his deflated lungs to the floor. His arm had been blown clean off, and now his chest was caving in, but the most painful thing of all was that this new band was unknowingly bringing a Marash House spy into their ranks. She would be nursed to health, any initial confusion would be explained away by the head trauma, and in the end, Marash would successfully infiltrate another band of Upper Thieves.

The strangest thought ran through Bhirus's mind as he watched his fellow Uppers carry Vinia down the ramp to safety.

*Well, Vinia, I guess your God ended up saving you after all, and I have to say He's got a killer sense of humor on Him.*

"What about the Marash scum?" boomed a voice from directly above him. "Cage 'im or Kill 'im?"

"Kill him," came the Master's order.

There was a loud blast from—

*Once chance to earn his freedom—yet for Wil that means confronting his past. With a probationary officer monitoring his every move, he wonders if he will truly be given a second chance at life.*

# A FREE MAN
## JAKE TYSON

# CHAPTER ONE
# INDENTURED

The null was beautiful.

Wil Freeman had been born in the null. At least, that was what Uncle Paxon told him. Obviously, Wil didn't remember the moment of his birth, but his uncle had been there, aboard the damaged light freighter drifting across the null, millions of lightyears from the nearest habitable planet. They'd been close to *Nexus Seven-Two-One*— relatively close, in terms of astronomical distances—but with their engines damaged, they hadn't been able to cross into the in-between to get there.

Wil's mother had given birth to him on that damaged freighter and passed him off to his uncle. Shortly after, she had died, succumbing to injuries taken when the freighter had been hit by a volley from a Clerical Court fighter. Everyone else aboard had died, too. Everyone except Uncle Paxon and Wil. They'd made it to an escape pod and sent a distress beacon, and it wasn't long before the Clerical Court's officers had returned to take them in.

They'd been pirates, Wil's family had, and for that, his mother had been sentenced to death before he even got to meet her.

"You okay?" Mona asked.

Wil glanced up from the thick glass viewport. Mona had her thick, dark hair in an intricate braid thrown over her shoulder—the only practical way to wear hair that long aboard a space vessel.

"Yeah, fine. Just ready to get this show on the road."

"You don't have to do this, you know."

Was that supposed to sound sympathetic? Wil snorted. She said that like his only other option wasn't prison.

"I do, actually. Terms of my release, and all that. Shouldn't you know that? You're my babysitter, after all."

Mona bristled, and it gave Wil the slightest jolt of amusement. Mona was a cleric of the Judicial Clerical Court, and proud of it. The uniform complimented her dark brown skin, but he'd never tell her that. He wasn't supposed to like her. She was here to make sure he complied with the Court's terms, not to be his friend.

"Well, if you don't want to go back to your cell, then I guess we'd better get moving," Mona said.

Wil looked back out at the stars. Their ship was currently docked at one of the stations orbiting Protocol Alpha, the port side of their vessel facing out toward the null. Somewhere out there, orbiting one of those distant pinpricks of light, was their destination. And the sooner they got there, the better.

"That's what I'm saying." Wil strode out of the ship's main hold and toward the cockpit. "Do we have clearance to take off yet, or what?"

"They're doing last-minute preparations, making sure the tracking device is in place and that Gamma and Delta Order forces are assembled to follow." Mona slipped by him and dropped into the pilot's seat. Now it was Wil's turn to bristle. "What's wrong?"

"It's just . . . " Wil frowned. "I would've preferred to fly."

"Part of the deal, Freeman. I fly, because if you do, what's stopping you from taking us to some out-of-the-way planet and ditching me there?"

Wil pointed to his wrist, where a tracking chip had been embedded. "Uh, this?"

Wil's surname had never seemed so ironic to him. Freeman was about the farthest thing from what he was. Even out of prison, he had a tracker on his ship and a tracker in his body. Sure, they said they'd remove it once the mission was done. Wil had met many people in his twenty-seven years that insisted the Federated Nations, that the Judicial Clerical Court, were a good and benevolent government. Wil wasn't sure he believed it.

"Still not taking chances," Mona said in a sing-song tone. "Sorry, Wil. But just give me the right coordinates, let me fly there, and once it's all over, you're free to go."

"And I get this ship, right?" Wil patted the console. "Right?"

The *Centennial* was technically the property of the Court, but he'd negotiated a ship as part of their agreement. This one would do nicely. A sleek *Cherubim*-class blockade runner, the *Centennial* was a beautiful silvery dagger of a vessel. He'd fallen in love with it at first sight. It had to be his.

"I don't think they said this ship, specifically." Mona bit her lip. "I can try to talk them into it, though."

"Really?"

"Yeah, sure. You're doing us a big favor, after all."

Wil narrowed his eyes. "Why are you trying to help me, Mona?"

"I think all beings deserve second chances, that's all."

"What's that, a religious thing?"

"Partly." Mona shrugged. "My friend, Cleric Samuels, says not to let evil invade our order and hearts and that we should offer grace. But partly it's also just my faith in people."

"Ah. I don't got that."

"No?"

"No. Because if you don't put faith in people, then people never let you down." Wil finally accepted that he wouldn't get to fly and dropped into the navigator's chair. "I've had way too many bad experiences for blind trust."

"Maybe you're just trusting the wrong people."

Now it was Wil's turn to bristle. "Whatever."

# CHAPTER TWO
## CALM

The pseudo-motion weirdness of the in-between never ceased to unsettle Mona Garrett. She and her family had spent most of their lives on Protocol Alpha, not traveling into space except on a few special occasions. Anytime they had made such a trip, it had been aboard a passenger vessel where they were seated in an inner compartment of the ship, without a view of the null. When Mona had joined the Court, she'd had to teach herself not to get space sick whenever she saw the in-between from the cockpit.

Most of the time, she just tried not to pay attention to it. Most ships had a viewport darkener that turned the glass opaque, keeping the pilots from having to stare into the in-between. It wasn't often used, though; pilots preferred to have a constant view of what was going on outside, in case they needed to react quickly. So, Mona got into the practice of keeping the viewport transparent. Better to learn to cope with the in-between than to have the viewport darkened and run into an emergency.

Problem was, there wasn't much to take her mind off it today. Wil was, unsurprisingly, giving her the silent treatment, and she couldn't connect her devices to the 'net while the ship was in the in-between. She'd pre-downloaded a few holo-novels to pass the time, but she felt awkward reading while Wil was just . . . sitting there next to her.

She hoped his coordinates were legit. For his sake, she truly wanted this to work. She believed he had a lot of potential that he hadn't allowed to blossom because of his lifestyle. This agreement with the Court was a second chance—third, really—for him to get his life together.

Mona didn't know a lot about Wil beyond what had been provided by her superiors in the Gamma Order. He had practically been born in the prison system; only three days old when he and his uncle, the infamous Paxon Harkness, had been processed. Of course, being an infant, he hadn't been incarcerated himself. He'd been given to a foster family until Harkness served out his sentence, at which point the uncle had petitioned to get Wil back. Because of the Court's leniency, and the foster family's attention on their own newborn biological children, the request had been granted, and at nine years old, Wil had been returned to Harkness.

Only Harkness hadn't been rehabilitated. It wasn't long before he was terrorizing all of space again, Wil tagging along on every escapade. It had continued for years until, at seventeen, Wil had been caught by the Court and imprisoned.

Mona wasn't sure if Wil had been forced into a pirate's life by Harkness or if he'd chosen to continue in it after he was old enough to make his own decisions, but ten years later, here he was, agreeing to help the Court in exchange for his freedom. Maybe that was a good sign, or maybe Wil would go back to breaking intergalactic law as soon as he had a few thousand parsecs between him and Protocol Alpha, but either way, he was here.

"I'm . . . going to use the head." Mona rose. "I've got the navigation log synced with my personal communicator. If you try to change course, I'll know."

Wil snorted. "Okay."

Mona sighed and ducked out of the cockpit. If he was going to be stubborn, so be it. She didn't need to be his friend, although she wouldn't mind a little pleasant conversation. What was the harm in that? Apparently, to him, a lot.

She reached for the clasp to remove her holster and hesitated. If she left her weapon out here, Wil might get a hold of it. She wanted to trust him, and she doubted he'd do anything to ruin his chances, but better safe than sorry. She left the holster until she stepped into the restroom and closed the door behind her. Then she removed it and hung it on the hook inside the door.

She caught her hands trembling as she lowered them from the hook. She clenched them into fists to stop the shaking. *You can do this, Mona.* This mission wasn't going to be a breeze, by any means, but it was within her grasp. It had to be. Otherwise, why had her curator assigned her to it?

Five minutes later, she returned her holster to her belt and stepped out of the restroom. She was halfway back to the cockpit when the ship rumbled. Mona froze in her tracks. They were in the in-between. There shouldn't have been any turbulence. Any . . . well, anything. What could've caused that vibration? Had Wil dropped them back into the null? She rested her hand on her weapon.

"Uh, Mona?" Wil's voice came over the intercom. "You might want to get up here."

Her feet kicked into gear on their own accord. "What's wrong?"

Wil pointed out the viewport, which now showed the null rather than the in-between, as she entered the cockpit. "Meteor storm."

# CHAPTER THREE
## CHAOS

**W**il snapped his seat restraints and tightened them as much as he could. Of course, there would be a meteor storm! Nothing could ever be easy for Wil. Mona scrambled into her seat and grabbed the controls. He wondered if she knew how to fly well enough to avoid the erratic chunks of ice rocketing in every direction around them. Maybe he should offer to take the controls. Or maybe he should just take them.

"Hold on!" Mona jerked the ship left. "This is gonna be tight."

"You think?" Wil shouted.

He'd only been in one meteor storm before, when he'd been fourteen. Uncle Paxon had been flying, and he'd barely gotten them out of it. Uncle Paxon was one of the best pilots Wil had ever seen— maybe the best ever. From what Wil had seen of Mona's serviceable skills, she was nowhere near Paxon's level.

"Let me take the controls!" Wil shouted.

A meteor slashed the null in half in front of them, missing the *Centennial* by maybe a dozen meters. Way, way too close. Mona's eyes were locked on the viewport, her hands turning the controls this way and that as they bobbed between the projectiles. Wil clutched his armrests and glanced over at Mona. Had she even heard his question?

"I'm not allowed to let you take the controls for any reason!" Mona finally replied. "I'd be in big trouble if I did!"

"Bigger trouble than getting smashed to bits by a meteor?"

Wil knew the pitch of his voice was rising, that he probably sounded hysterical. He couldn't bring himself to care. Some people wanted to die with dignity. Not Wil. If Wil died, it would be kicking and screaming and clutching for life to his last breath. Nothing was going to take him down the easy way. No, sir.

"Look, I'm a better pilot than any one of you curators or custodians! And, more importantly, *I don't want to die!*"

Despite the severity of the situation, he saw the corners of Mona's mouth curl up. *Is she . . . is she smiling?* Wil resisted the urge to reach over and smack her. This was no time for laughing!

The ship rumbled with an impact. "Mona!"

She growled. "Okay, fine. Take the controls. Get us out of this!"

Wil lurched forward and grabbed the copilot's controls. Mona flicked a switch to transfer power over to him, and he weaved around an oncoming meteor. Adrenaline rushed through him, filling his chest with a burst of excitement. It had been too long since he'd flown. *Ten years . . .* he shoved the thought aside and focused on the danger ahead.

The flight was like a dance. Wil let his instincts guide him, taking him between every large ice rock on the meteor storm. Mona was quiet, or else he'd tuned her out completely, because all he heard was the rumble of the engines; all he felt was the hum of the ship behind the controls.

Ten agonizing minutes later, the ship floated in the null, the meteors behind them. Wil slumped back in his seat and sighed in relief. He reached up to run a hand through his dark hair and found it matted to his head with sweat. He looked over at Mona. She was staring at him, her eyes wide.

"That was incredible."

He smiled—and cursed himself when he realized it was genuine. "Thanks."

"You're welcome. So, what happened? Why did we get pulled out of the in-between like that? I've never known it to happen before."

"Most ships have a self-preservation subroutine. If anything unexpected is in the path of the charged in-between route, it automatically drops us back into the null. Good thing it did, or we would've plowed through that storm at faster-than-light speeds. There wouldn't have been enough of the *Centennial* left to scoop into a trash receptacle." Wil unbuckled and stretched, popping his back. "But we're safe now. The coordinates should still be in, so you can resume the journey. We should be at our destination in no time."

"You going somewhere?"

"Check the systems for damage. No telling what a few of those impacts might've done. If we end up in a battle, we don't want shields or weapons to fail at a bad time, do we?"

Mona's brow furrowed. "You think this'll end in a battle?"

As if it could end any other way? "Oh, yeah. For what you're wanting me to do . . . a battle is inevitable."

# CHAPTER FOUR
## DELIBERATION

As the ship returned to the in-between, Mona slumped back in her seat. That had been way too close. She hated to admit it, but if Wil hadn't taken over flying, she wasn't sure they'd have made it out of there in one piece. Flying had never been her strongest suit. Shooting? She could do that. Give her a weapon and a target, and it didn't matter the distance between them; she'd find a way to hit it. But flying . . . well, she was glad he'd been there.

His words as he'd left the cockpit resonated in the confined space, reminding her of their ultimate objective. She supposed she'd been naive to think this could end any way other than with a fight. Maybe it was that hope she'd told him about earlier. Maybe she'd just believed that it would all be resolved with a simple surrender, and that no one would have to get hurt. But that didn't seem likely at all.

In which case, she might just end up having to show off her shooting skills.

Mona rose from her seat. The odds of them having another freak accident like the storm were next to zero, so she felt safe leaving the autopilot to get them through the rest of the journey in the in-between. It would alert her when they were two minutes out from returning to the null. Stepping out into the hallway, Mona followed in Wil's path.

Wil looked up from a diagnostics panel. "Thought you trusted me."

"Huh? Oh, I do."

"Then why're you following me out here? Think I'm going to sabotage the ship? Then I'd die, too, you know."

"I didn't think that for a second." Mona settled on the main hold's couch. "I am curious, though . . . do you have any reservations?"

"About the mission? Of course, I do. What you're asking me to do—"

"We're asking you to protect the Federated Nations."

"You're asking me to betray my uncle." Wil whirled on her. "Don't pretend like it's anything more noble than that."

Mona clamped her mouth shut. Wil turned back to the diagnostics panel and scrolled with one finger. Mona reached for her device and pulled up one of her novels. She started reading, but ten minutes in she found that she'd reread the same page four times and still hadn't retained any of it. She sighed and closed down the device, setting it on the table in front of her.

"You know your uncle hurts people, right?"

Wil looked at her, then back at the panel, and sighed. "I know. I know he does. I know I used to. But it's just life, you know? We'd been abandoned by the Federated Nations, left to our own devices, and so we did what we had to do to survive. It wasn't glamorous, but it was better than dying."

"You really think the Nations abandoned you?"

"Yes!"

Mona blinked at the venom in his tone. "They didn't, you know. I've heard the story. It was your uncle who turned traitor.

He used his position for personal gain, and when the Court found out, they—"

"They ruined his life."

"They protected the innocent. Your uncle and everyone who sided with him were supposed to be arrested, but they fled. Became pirates."

"Including my mother."

"Yes."

Wil lapsed back into silence. Mona suspected he'd always known the story but had told himself that his uncle's interpretation was more accurate. She couldn't blame him. Like her, he was looking for the best in people. Only he was only looking for it in one person: his uncle. She empathized.

"So, why'd you agree to help us, then?" she pressed. "If you don't think he's wrong."

"Because I wanted out of prison."

Mona pursed her lips. Maybe, but there had to be more to it than that. To sell out the man who'd raised him from the time he was nine, through the formative teenage years . . . that took more than just a promise of freedom. Wil seemed loyal to Harkness, loyal to a fault, and more than willing to do time if it meant his uncle's freedom.

"I think you're lying." Mona crossed the hold to stand next to Wil. "I think you would only turn against him if you had a really good reason."

Wil looked up at her—and the destination alarm went off. *Saved by the bell.* Mona turned and strode for the cockpit. Her stomach worked itself into knots. If they were really here, then it was time. There was no turning back now. They were about to meet Paxon Harkness's pirate fleet—and with any luck, bring it down for good.

# CHAPTER FIVE
# REVELATION

Wil swallowed the lump in his throat as he followed Mona to the cockpit. She'd struck closer to the truth than he would've liked. What right did she have to do that, anyway? She didn't know him. Of course, he had his reasons for agreeing to help the Judicial Clerical Court bring down his uncle. But those reasons were his own, and none of her business.

They dropped into orbit over a beautiful blue planet, pockmarked with the occasional green-and-brown island. This planet, Litore Prime, was renowned for its beaches. It was no surprise that a crew of wealthy pirates would settle there, whenever they weren't in space—it was the perfect place to spend their excess wealth in revelry and debauchery.

Mona whistled. "It's gorgeous."

"It's his home." Wil ground his jaw. "Give me the transmitter."

"You sure this is the best way to go about it?"

"You got any other ideas on how to get a whole fleet of partying pirates back into space in a hurry?" Wil grabbed the transmitter from her. "Trust me, this will work."

*Trust me.* He blinked at his own words. After all the flak he'd given her for being too trusting, now he was asking her to do just that. And he had before, too, in the meteor storm.

He hesitated before pressing the button to open a line. "Mona, why do you trust me?"

"Well, like I said." She shrugged. "I believe everyone deserves another chance. I might be wrong about you, but I don't think I am."

"Let's hope you're right." Wil clicked the transmit button. "This is Wil Freeman calling Paxon Harkness on all channels. Uncle Pax, you hear me? This is Wil. Repeat, this is Wil. I need help—fast."

Mona blinked at him, but Wil held up a steadying hand. She settled back, her eyes never leaving him. He noticed her hand falling near her weapon. *Smart.* But he didn't believe she could bring herself to shoot him, even if he did betray her. She was too nice.

"Repeat, this is Wil Freeman calling Paxon Harkness. Are you there, Uncle Pax?"

The receiver crackled. "Wil! What in space are you doing here? And is that a Court vessel? I nearly had you blown out of orbit, boy!"

*That's Uncle Pax, all right.* "It's a Court vessel, all right, Uncle Pax. I escaped from their prison, stole this ship, and fought my way out—took a bit of doing, too. My reentry panels have been damaged, and my shields are shot, so I'm kind of stranded up here. The ship will never make landfall. Not to mention, I've probably got two or three patrol ships on my trail that could come out of the in-between anytime now. So, could you send someone up here to get me?"

"Patrol ships? Boy, what's wrong with you, leading them here?"

Wil grimaced. So much for a happy reunion. He glanced at Mona, saw the pity in her eyes. Finally, he swallowed and depressed the transmitter again. Here went nothing. This had to work.

"I didn't know where else to go, Uncle Pax. I'm sorry. Listen, I'm sure one or two of your ships would be enough to fight 'em off . . . just send a rescue team to get me off this death trap and leave a squadron up here to fight back. We'll be fine."

"Are you telling me what to do, Wil?" Paxon growled. "I ain't taking chances. I'm launching the whole fleet. We'll be up there to get you soon enough. Just sit tight and use this time to think about the mistakes you made—about how you could've ruined me with your stupidity."

The line went dead. Wil exhaled and set the transmitter down on the console. Mona was still staring at him, eyes wide.

"What?" He shrugged. "You thought Pax and I were one big happy family? The guy left me behind to be arrested so he could escape. That's how I ended up in prison. You think he was doing me a kindness, taking me from that foster family? He just wanted someone to pickpocket who people wouldn't suspect. Paxon don't love me. I'm just a tool."

"That's why you agreed to help us take him down."

"That's why." Wil rose. "Now, I need to go see about turning our shields back on before all the shooting starts?"

"Turn the shields—wait, you mean they're really down?"

"Yep. Had to make it convincing in case he had his crew scan us. I'll be standing by to turn them on when you give the word. Will the Court's forces be here soon?"

Mona nodded. "Anytime now. And Harkness won't know what hit him."

"I sure hope not. Oh, one thing, Mona?"

"What's that?"

"Part of my agreement with the Court—you and I are taking the kill shot on Pax's ship."

Wil stormed out of the cockpit, ready to have this over with.

# CHAPTER SIX
## COUNTDOWN

**M**ona remained in the cockpit, stunned by the revelations Wil had dropped on her. Was he really so bloodthirsty for his uncle's life? It was understandable, she supposed. He'd been betrayed by the person who was supposed to be his caretaker. It almost made Mona glad they'd be taking the kill shot. She never celebrated loss of life, but someone like Paxon . . .

Someone like Paxon had to be brought down for the greater good.

She glanced at the counter next to the pilot's controls. The Court fleet would arrive in less than five minutes. Harkness's ships were just starting to show up as dark shapes against the surface of the planet. In contrast to the sleek Court ships, the pirate vessels were all jagged edges, terrifying shapes of menace and murder.

Mona felt her blood run cold. "Here they come, Wil."

"His big ships will get into position first," Wil called. "I reckon he won't send a rescue ship for us until all his defenses are lined up. It's the smart thing to do, tactically."

"But then the fleet will be walking into an ambush."

"Nah. Pax is expecting a few fighters, maybe a light cruiser or two. When the whole armada appears, the pirates will be thrown into chaos."

"I hope you're right."

"Trust me. I know my uncle. He's overconfident, but more than that, he doesn't think I'm worth sending more than a skeleton crew to catch. The idea that a whole force would be on my tail . . . it's too far out for him to conceive. And he doesn't think I'm smart enough to betray him, either."

Wil said it with a lighthearted tone, but Mona sensed the pain behind it. How must that have felt, growing up with someone who treated him like an inferior mind? An inferior being?

"I'm sorry, Wil."

"Don't be. I don't need pity."

The timer clicked down to ten seconds. The pirate fleet was positioned now, five huge battleships with two cruisers flanking each. Mona guessed the pirates probably had fifty single-man fighters to lead the attack. The armada would have twice that, and the pirate's biggest battleship couldn't compare to the size of the Court's monstrosities.

Five seconds. "Here we go, Wil . . . "

With a ripple of motion, the Judicial Clerical Court's armada appeared. Seconds later, the space all around Litore Prime lit up with cannonfire.

# CHAPTER SEVEN
# JUSTICE

At Mona's call, Wil flipped the shields back to full and cantered down the hallway to the cockpit. Mona already had the *Centennial* in motion, weaving through the laser blasts erupting from ship to ship. Wil's eyes widened at the size of the Court's battleships. He'd never seen them up close before. They were . . . enormous. Even Uncle Pax's ships didn't compare. Wil shook himself from his shock and buckled in.

"Wil!" Pax shouted over the comm line. "You stupid boy! You said it was just a few light ships! This is the whole fleet!"

Wil grabbed the transmitter. "Oh, did I? My mistake."

Paxon started cussing Wil out, so Wil shut off the line. He'd reopen it again later, when he was ready to deliver the killing blow. For now, he had pirate ships to shoot down. He grabbed the controls to the *Centennial*'s guns and opened fire. Two pirate fighters erupted immediately. In the close space around the planet, there were almost too many ships to navigate around. Every shot was all but guaranteed to hit its mark. Wil just hoped he didn't hit any Court fighters by mistake. Not that he'd lose too much sleep over it, but he did still want to be on their good side by the end of this.

"Which one is Harkness'?" Mona asked.

"He'll be on his capital ship, the *Harrier*." He pointed. "It's the one with the bloodred paint on the hull."

"We can't destroy that ship with our guns!"

"I know. We'll need to let your battleships whittle it down. Then we'll make our run on the bridge and blow Pax into the in-between."

Mona chewed her lip. "You'll have to do it."

"Huh?"

"You'll have to fly. I'm not good enough to strafe a battleship at close enough range to hit the bridge. I'll end up crashing us. But what I can do is shoot. If you can fly in that close, I'll be able to blast the bridge. We'll kill Pax together and end this for good."

Wil clenched his jaw. He'd wanted to be the one shooting when Pax died, but . . . it was a good point. He didn't want to die along with his uncle. He supposed flying the ship that blew Pax up was the next best thing. Nodding, he switched over to the pilot controls as Mona reprogrammed the console to give herself control of the guns. Wil darted around a cruiser and gave Mona an opening at its engines. Before the cruiser had exploded, they were on their way to the next target.

"Wonder how Pax is feeling now?"

Wil reached over to turn the transmitter back on. Instantly, they were met by more shouted curses. Wil glanced over at Mona, whose eyes were wide. He chuckled. Pax had always had a mouth on him.

"You hear me, boy?" Pax roared. "I'm coming out there to take you down myself!"

*Oh, boy.*

"What's he mean?" Mona asked.

"His personal fighter. The *Crimson Reaper.*" Wil's heart sank. "Pax taught me how to fly. He's the best there is . . . I don't know if I can outfly him."

"You can. Just get me a lock, and I'll blow him away."

"Okay. Thanks, Mona. You're . . . a good friend."

She smiled. "You're welcome."

Wil spun the *Centennial* around and aimed for the *Harrier.* It didn't take long to spot the double-dagger shape of the *Crimson Reaper.* In seconds, Pax's fighter shot down three Court fighters and blew the mounted guns off one of the cruisers. Pax was good, all right. Maybe he'd even gotten better in the last ten years.

Didn't matter. He was still going down.

"Here we go."

Wil shot toward Paxon, dodging all other oncoming ships. Mona blasted a few that tried to hug their tail. Wil was impressed. She hadn't lied about her shooting skills. He just hoped they were enough to finish Pax. He was headed right for them now, his red fighter spinning like a drill through space.

Pax fired a rocket.

"Uh, Mona . . . "

"Got it!"

She fired, blowing the missile out of the sky. Pax's fighter flew through the explosion and opened up with lasers. The *Centennial's* shields took the shots full on. Mona fired on the *Crimson Reaper*— Wil arced to the right at the last second to avoid a collision. The *Centennial's* internal alarms wailed, warning of low power to the shields. Wil brought the ship around. They wouldn't get too many more shots at this . . .

"Watch it!" Mona shouted.

She fired again before they'd completed their turn, destroying another missile. Wil spotted Pax's ship and aimed for it. Pax came at them again, still spinning. It was his signature move, meant to strike fear into his opponents. Wil had to admit, it was intimidating.

Not to Mona, though. She was still firing, lasers peppering the *Crimson Reaper*. But Pax was firing back, and their shields were dropping by the second. Wil spared a glance at the console. Ten percent. The ships crossed paths again, and Wil went into another turn. He reached over to mute the alarm. It wasn't helping them now.

"This is it," he said. "We won't survive another turn."

"Then we'll finish him on this one." Mona tightened her grip on the controls. "Let's blow him out of the sky."

Wil grinned despite himself. He felt better, having her here with him. Killing Pax alone would've put him in a dark place. Now, it didn't feel so much like vengeance. It felt like . . . like protecting all the people Pax would hurt if he wasn't taken down. It felt like justice. Pax had to die, but Wil didn't have to let doing it consume him.

The ships faced each other again. Wil ran his tongue across his dry lips. *Whatever God Mona prays to . . . please let us live through this.*

"I should've left you on that ship to rot with your mother," Paxon growled.

"Maybe you should've." Wil nodded to Mona. "Guess we'll never know."

She fired. The shot ripped through the canopy of the *Crimson Reaper*. In an instant, the fighter exploded into atoms. And just like that, Paxon Harkness was gone.

# CHAPTER EIGHT
# FREEDOM

**W**il stood with his hands behind his back, looking out again at the null. Several judges were in the courtroom behind him, deliberating the success of the mission. Wil wasn't worried. He knew there was only one way it could go. Pax's fleet had gone down with minimal casualties to the Armada. Federated Nations space was now free of a pirate scourge, and Wil had been a key part of making it happen.

"You okay?"

Wil smiled and turned. Mona stood behind him, just as she had before their mission. She had a new rank badge added to her uniform; she'd received a promotion for helping take down Pax. She deserved it.

"I'm good. Killing Pax wasn't . . . well, it wasn't as satisfying as I thought it would be, but it had to be done."

"And now you're free."

"Well." He gestured to the door. "Assuming they're satisfied with my service."

"They will be. You did great. I put in a word for you on saving us from that meteor storm." Mona stepped up beside him. "I think you're a good man, Wil Freeman."

"Thanks. I'm trying to be."

"You ever think about becoming a curator?"

"Eh . . . not for me, I don't think. I need a job where I can be more free."

"Well, if you change your mind."

The door to the chamber opened, and a bailiff gestured for Wil to enter. He nodded and stepped in that direction.

"Hey, Wil!" He stopped and glanced back at Mona's call. "Wherever you go, just know you can always count on me as a friend."

He smiled and strode into the courtroom. He hadn't heard their decision yet, but for the first time ever, Wil finally felt like a free man.

# THE END

# IF YOU ENJOYED *INTO THE UNKNOWN,* CHECK OUT THESE BOOKS. . .

## DANIEL PEYTON

*Remnant*

WWW.FACEBOOK.COM/DANIELPEYTONAUTHOR

## ERIC LANDFRIED

*Solitary Man*

*Conflicted Man*

WWW.ERICLANDFRIED.COM

## LAUREN SMYTH

*Stories of the Night*

*Made for Mercy*

*With Love from the Past*

WWW.ERICLANDFRIED.COM

## P.S. PATTON

*The Withering*

WWW.PSPATTON.COM

## Daphne Self

*When Legends Rise*
*What Legends Become* (Coming Soon)
**WWW.AUTHORDAPHNESELF.BLOGSPOT.COM**

## Allen Steadham

*Mindfire*
*Jordan's World*
*Jordan's Arrow*
*Jordan's Deliverance*
**WWW.ALLENSTEADHAM.COM**

## Jake Tyson

*Vigilante's Light*
*Freedom's Fight*
*Heroes' Might*
**WWW.CREATINGFORCREATOR.WORDPRESS.COM**

# MORE FICTION FROM AMBASSADOR INTERNATIONAL

Elaine Smith is content with her life as a widow in the small, coastal town of Sabal Palms. She enjoys her time with friends, and she enjoys writing stories and devotionals, despite the advice of her friends. When a southern squall hits the coast, Elaine's abandoned writings start showing up in the most mysterious places. Can God actually use Elaine's trash to become someone else's treasure? Is there more to her writings than she even realizes?

After Catherine Reed's husband dies, she moves back home in order to accept a new position as the teacher for the town's one-room schoolhouse. Samuel Harris has suffered his own loss and guilt has burdened him ever since. When his old flame comes back to town, he wonders if they can find healing together . . .

King Solomon is well-known as a wise man and the wealthiest king to have ever lived. But with great power often comes great corruption, and Solomon was no exception—including his collection of wives and concubines. But who were these women? What was life like for them in Solomon's harem? S.A. Jewell dives into a deeper part of Solomon's kingdom and shows how God is always faithful, even when we may doubt His plan.